the manny

the manny

Sarah L. Thomson

DUTTON CHILDREN'S BOOKS • NEW YORK

DUTTON CHILDREN'S BOOKS

A division of Penguin Young Readers Group
Published by the Penguin Group
Penguin Group (USA) Inc., 375 Hudson Street, New York, New York 10014, U.S.A.
Penguin Group (Canada), 10 Alcorn Avenue, Toronto, Ontario, Canada M4V 3B2
(a division of Pearson Penguin Canada Inc.)
Penguin Books Ltd, 80 Strand, London WC2R 0RL, England
Penguin Ireland, 25 St Stephen's Green, Dublin 2, Ireland (a division of Penguin Books Ltd)
Penguin Group (Australia), 250 Camberwell Road, Camberwell, Victoria 3124, Australia
(a division of Pearson Australia Group Pty Ltd)
Penguin Books India Pvt Ltd, 11 Community Centre,
Panchsheel Park, New Delhi - 110 017, India
Penguin Group (NZ), Cnr Airborne and Rosedale Roads, Albany, Auckland 1310, New Zealand
(a division of Pearson New Zealand Ltd)
Penguin Books (South Africa) (Pty) Ltd, 24 Sturdee Avenue,
Rosebank, Johannesburg 2196, South Africa
Penguin Books Ltd, Registered Offices: 80 Strand, London WC2R 0RL, England

LIBRARY OF CONGRESS CATALOGING-IN-PUBLICATION DATA
Thomson, Sarah L.
The manny/by Sarah L. Thomson.—1st ed.
p. cm.
Summary: A sixteen-year-old New Yorker looks forward to his summer job as a manny, or "male
nanny," to an affluent couple's four-year-old in the Hamptons.
ISBN 0-525-47413-7 (alk. paper)
[1. Nannies—Fiction. 2. Dating (Social customs)—Fiction. 3. Vacations—Fiction.
4. Hamptons (N.Y.)—Fiction.] I. Title.
PZ7.T3813Man 2005
[Fic]—dc22 2004022233

Published in the United States by Dutton Children's Books,
a division of Penguin Young Readers Group
345 Hudson Street, New York, New York 10014
www.penguin.com/youngreaders
Designed by Jason Henry
Printed in USA * First Edition
1 3 5 7 9 10 2 6 4 2

For Trina, who let the neighbor's dog in;
for Jennifer, who jumped off the dock;
and for Michele, who came up with the idea

the manny

MY NAME IS JUSTIN BLAKEWELL, and I'm sixteen years old. And I'm a nanny.

Fine, go ahead and laugh. Everybody else does.

But tell me one thing: can you come up with a better summer job? Flipping burgers? Standing over a vat of boiling grease, while wearing a stupid polyester hat, getting a face full of zits for minimum wage? No thanks.

Taking tickets at the Cineplex? See above re: hat.

Mowing lawns? I live in New York City. There are no lawns.

No, the nanny thing is definitely the way to go. Although I believe, technically speaking, the term is "manny." (Get it? Male nanny? Riotously funny, isn't it?) If you've been keeping up with things, you'll know that this is starting to be a real trend, hiring guys to look after little kids. I hear a manny even showed up on *Friends*.

I was explaining all this to my best friend, Alex. This was about the point when he started to fall over laughing.

"You're gonna be a *nanny?*" he gasped, wiping tears of laughter from his eyes and ignoring the fine distinction between *nanny* and *manny* that I had just so carefully explained. "You can't be a nanny. *Girls* are nannies."

This is a fairly typical reaction. It shows you that Alex, along with most of my other friends, fails to grasp an essential piece of the nanny picture.

Dillon, however, gets it. Dillon's another friend of mine.

"That's right, stupid," he said. He looked at Alex with pity. "*Girls* are nannies."

Picture this. Me at the park with little Aspen Jeremy Belton, age four. It's a nice sunny day. Little kids are swinging, climbing the jungle gym, whacking their friends over the head with shovels in the sandbox. And all of them are being watched by nannies. Nannies who are girls.

And then there's me. Tying Aspen's shoelaces. Picking him up when he falls down. Mr. Sensitive. Mr. Caring. Mr. I-Love-Kids-I-Can't-Wait-to-Have-a-Bushel-of-My-Own-Someday.

Girls *love* that sort of stuff.

And to top it all off, I won't just be watching little Aspen at the park down the street. Nope, I'll be at the Beltons' house in the Hamptons. Skipping out on the hot, sticky summer in New York for a month on the beaches of Long Island. Where there are not only girls in bikinis, there are *rich* girls in bikinis.

This is going to be a great summer.

Chapter
2

THE BELTONS' CONDO on Central Park West is up so high, my ears are popping as we go up in the elevator. We're headed for the thirty-ninth floor, but my stomach got left somewhere in the basement.

It's nothing like the elevator in the building where my mom and I live. That one is so old and creaky it's faster to take the stairs. This one whooshes us up like it was designed by NASA.

See, what I said earlier was a bit of an exaggeration. Technically speaking, I'm not a manny yet. I'm a manny-to-be. I still have to be interviewed by Aspen's parents. And my mom has to meet them, to be sure they're not whacked-out psychos intent on luring her only child off to the Hamptons for dark rituals in which small animals are sacrificed.

We don't, in case you were wondering, know the Beltons socially. This is how I got the interview:

Mr. Belton knows the principal of my school, Mr. Muñoz. Mr. Muñoz is dating my English teacher, Ms. Lasky. And I don't let this out to the world at large, but for the last several months I've been watching Ms. Lasky's two little monsters (twins Ian and Michael, age five) every other Saturday night. It cuts into my social life, but on the other hand, it gives me enough money to go out on the weekends when I'm not playing with Legos and building forts out of pillows.

The Beltons asked Mr. Muñoz if he knew anybody who wanted a summer job taking care of a kid. Mr. Muñoz asked Ms. Lasky if *she* knew anybody. Since I haven't lost, damaged, or murdered either of her boys in the course of four months, and since she knew I was looking for work, Ms. Lasky told him that she knew me.

So that's how we got here this evening, headed up in this space-age elevator that seems set to go straight into the stratosphere.

I'm not worried about the interview. I mean, how hard can it be? After Ian and Michael, who like to gang up on me, one kid at a time should be a breeze. As long as I don't look like a drug addict or flash any gang signs, I figure I've got this job in my pocket.

There are mirrors all around the elevator. I check to make sure my hair's still in place. There's a piece in front that always wants to stick up, but I glued it down with some gel before I left home. It's still where it should be. I take a look at the rest of me while I'm there. Regular-looking guy, not a knockout but not a cause for shame, either. Not as skinny as I was two years ago. I think I look a little older than sixteen. Chinos pressed. Belt buckled. Shirt tucked in. Attention to detail counts when meeting prospective employers.

Then I catch sight of my mom in the mirror.

She came straight from her job, so she's still wearing work clothes. A pink skirt and jacket, nylons, the same black shoes she wears every day. She always looks a little strange to me like that. At home, she changes into jeans and a T-shirt first thing. When I was little, she says, I would burst into tears at the sight of her in a suit, since it meant she was going away.

She's not doing anything. She's not fixing her lipstick or fussing with her hair. But that's not so weird. My mom's one of the few females I know who doesn't go into repair mode at the sight of a mirror. What's weird is her face. She doesn't look worried. Or cheerful. Or even bored. She doesn't look like she's there at all. She looks like she's doing long division in her head.

"Uh . . . Mom?" I just want to make sure she's here on this planet with me.

But before she can turn and look my way, the elevator stops. A bell chimes. It sounds like we're being called to prayer in a Buddhist monastery. A soothing voice announces that we have reached the thirty-ninth floor. I wouldn't have been surprised if it had wished us a pleasant incarnation.

The sound seems to wake my mom up. "Okay," she says, coming back down to earth and giving me a quick, fake smile. "Here we go."

I wonder if my mother is more nervous about this than I am.

That starts to make *me* nervous.

The trick is not to show it. Be nervous all you like, but look cool. Smooth and suave. Don't talk. This is key. Lots of people start to babble when they get a little jumpy. Dead giveaway. Smile, nod, and shut up. Nobody ever looked stupid for what they *didn't* say.

I ring the bell of 39A and smooth my hair down just before the door opens.

"Justin? Mrs. Blakewell?" The guy who opens the door is

tall, wearing jeans and a gray shirt, no shoes, purple socks. Whatever's in the glass he's holding looks like water, but I bet it's not. "I'm Kevin Belton," he says. "Come in."

Acres of polished wood floor. Dark red rugs. Bushy green plants everywhere. A painting on the wall of a really sick-looking guy staring out of a window. His face appears to be melting.

"You like it?" Mr. Belton says, when he notices where I'm looking.

"Um . . . huh . . . yeah," I say. Oh, great. What happened to smooth and suave? What happened to shutting up and nodding?

"I don't either," Mr. Belton says. "But Gayle loves it. Gayle!" He yells toward the kitchen. "They're here!"

"Coming!"

Mrs. Belton comes out of the kitchen with a plate of cheese in one hand and a bottle of beer in the other. We all sit down on a couple of couches near the windows. While we're eating cheese and looking out over Central Park, we agree that my mom can call the Beltons Kevin and Gayle, that they can call her Linda, that she'd love a glass of white wine, that I'd like a Coke, and that the oozy white cheese with the spots of green and blue mold is delicious.

Actually, my opinion isn't asked about the cheese. Which is a good thing. Because my opinion is that it looks like Silly Putty somebody left at the back of the fridge for a couple of years, and there's no way I'm putting it in my mouth.

My mom and the Beltons are now talking about the subway, which is a thing New Yorkers do. Every time you get anywhere, you have to explain to people how you got there.

Now, if somebody were to say, "I strapped on my hang glider and took a leap off the Empire State Building, then hung a left at Thirty-second," I would be interested. But since everybody I know walks down into a hole in the ground, gets on a train, and eventually walks up out of a different hole, I don't get why we have to spend so much time discussing it.

"We had to change at Columbus Circle," my mom is saying. "And the platform was so crowded, I thought we wouldn't catch the C train . . ."

Yawn.

"All right, then, Justin," Mrs. Belton says all of a sudden. From somewhere, she's picked up a pad of paper and a pencil. She doesn't wear glasses, but if she did, I bet she'd be looking at me over the top of them right now.

"You've had some experience with child care, is that right?"

I smile, nod, and shut up.

"Tell us about that, why don't you?"

"Um, yeah. Yes. I've been babysitting for my English teacher since the winter. Every other week. She's got two boys. Twins. Five." What happened? It's like my vocal chords got stuck and now I can't speak a sentence with more than one word in it.

"And how much do you know about first aid?"

First aid? Ms. Lasky never asks me anything like this. She just scribbles down her cell phone number and tells me where the kids' pajamas are.

"Well, we did first aid in health this year," I say, hoping desperately that she's not going to ask me to apply a tourniquet or demonstrate CPR.

"And have you studied child development at all?"

Studied *what?*

"Gayle," Mr. Belton says. "He's sixteen. Why doesn't he just play with Aspen for a little bit so we can see how they get along?"

About then I become aware that someone is staring at me. I turn my head and see a pair of big brown eyes looking at me over the arm of the sofa, the kind of eyes that make women melt and start crooning stuff like, "Oh, aren't you a big boy?" He doesn't fool me, though. Eyes like that and a little round face can get you out of more trouble than a wallet full of cash.

"Aspen, honey," Mrs. Belton says. "Come over here and say hi."

The body that the eyes are attached to oozes around the corner of the couch and attaches itself to Mrs. Belton's chair.

"This is Aspen," Mrs. Belton says. "Say hi, sweetie."

The mouth moves, but if any sound comes out, I can't hear it.

My mom leans forward a little in her chair. "How old are you, Aspen?" she asks, smiling at him.

After serious thought, Aspen holds up three fingers.

"No, you're not three anymore," Mrs. Belton says. "How many?"

Slowly, like the hinge is rusty, the little finger unfolds and sticks up to join the other three.

"Aspen, this is Justin," Mr. Belton says. "Why don't you show Justin your room?"

Right. Time to show them how good I am with kids. My interviewing technique may be a little rusty, but my Lego skills are as sharp as ever.

"Yeah, Aspen, c'mon," I say, getting up. "Let's go see your toys."

Aspen leans harder, if possible, against his mom's chair. He doesn't move, but his head slowly tips back to look up at my face.

"He's a little shy," Mrs. Belton whispers, like Aspen can't hear. "Go on, honey, it's okay." And she pushes him gently away from her.

There's a tense moment when Aspen stands dead still and nobody says anything. What am I supposed to do if the kid doesn't like me? Will the interview end right here? Will I slink back down in the elevator and try to dig up a summer job at the corner deli? I'm trying to remember whether the guys behind the counter at the deli wear hats when, at last, Aspen slowly moves his feet and heads off down the hall. I follow him. Because we're going at a snail's pace, I can still hear the conversation behind me.

"Aspen . . . that's an unusual name," my mom says.

"Well, he was conceived there," Mrs. Belton says. "On a ski trip we took. It was such a special time . . ."

Chalk *that* up as #1 under Things I Really Didn't Want to Know.

Aspen's room is bigger than the whole apartment my mom and I share. Okay, I'm exaggerating, but not by much. Aspen just stands there, looking at the rug, which has pictures of roads and trucks and fire engines on it.

Okay, seriously, this can't be so hard. This kid isn't even sure how old he is. And I have no evidence that he can talk. As for me, I'm halfway through my high school education, and I make mostly A's (except for gym, which isn't my fault, because Coach Peterson is a Neanderthal with a whistle and a power complex). I'm smart enough to figure out something for a four-year-old to do.

I look around. There's a basket overflowing with stuffed animals, a bookshelf stacked with books, and a box of plastic action figures lying near the bed. He's got a fireman, a scuba diver, and a Navy SEAL, all of them looking like they'd be barred from the Olympics for steroid use. And . . . hey, over there, what's that?

"Legos!" I say. "You want to build with your Legos?"

After a very long moment, Aspen nods.

Saved.

This kid could start a Lego factory. Pretty soon we've got a launch pad/gas station/burger joint going. This is actually kind of fun. When I was a kid, there were never enough Legos to build something really good. You'd always run out of the cool pieces and be stuck with a handful of chewed-up white blocks that were only good for walls. But with this stash, we could build a scale model of the Eiffel Tower and have enough left over for a start on the Empire State Building.

"Okay, here's the rocket launcher," I say, sticking Legos together as fast as I can. "It needs to fuel up. You take it over there to the gas tank and fill 'er up, all right?"

Aspen does, with appropriate refueling noises, while I add a traffic control tower at the top of our masterpiece.

"This, this, this . . ." Aspen says. "This is the rocket. Okay?" He's holding out a big fat purple crayon.

A crayon? Sure, why not.

"Make it blast off, then," I tell him. And he does. With sound effects.

"Oh no!" I lob a few Legos at the rocket ship. "Meteor shower! Watch out, Captain!"

"Oh no oh no oh no!" Aspen yells.

"Emergency landing!" I shout.

And the spaceship *Purple Crayon* crash-lands on the carpet.

About then I look up. Mrs. Belton is standing in the doorway, smiling. Mr. Belton's looking over her shoulder.

How long have they been watching this?

"Justin," Mrs. Belton says. "We think you'd be great looking after Aspen. Would you like the job?"

We work out the terms. (Which means they tell me what the terms are and I nod.) In a week I'll be heading off to the Hamptons to be responsible for Aspen five hours a day, six days a week, Fridays off.

A little while later, when we're going down in the elevator, I notice that the piece of my hair in front is sticking up again.

Chapter 3

"THAT HAS GOT to be the sweetest deal in the history of summer jobs," Dillon says.

Dillon's on my bed, playing Snake on his cell phone. Alex is sitting on the floor, tossing a Wiffle ball into my trash can. I'm packing.

"I mean, how hard can it be, taking care of one little kid?" Dillon goes on. "People do this every day, all over the world. And *how* much are they going to pay you?"

"A hundred and fifty a week."

"And you get your own room?"

"Yeah."

"In the *Hamptons*?"

"Yeah."

"So what did you do in a former life to deserve this?"

"I dunno," I say. "Cured cancer or something."

I already know that Dillon's underestimating the difficulty of taking care of a little kid. My evenings with Ian and Michael, the tag team from hell, have taught me this. But I'm not about to argue with him because (a) I try not to talk much in public about what I do every other Saturday night, and (b) I think he's mostly right. This *is* a sweet deal. Sure, I know it's work taking care of a kid, but I can handle it. I've done it before. And it's only five hours a day, which means that even if I take out a healthy eight hours for sleep every night, I'll have eleven hours a day to work on the true objective of the summer—meeting girls.

I carefully shake the wrinkles out of my best blue shirt and lay it on top of the pile in my duffel bag.

"Saturday morning," Alex says, throwing the Wiffle ball, "the Beltons will be honking the horn out in the street and you'll still be sitting there saying, 'Oooh, should it be the gray or the blue shirt? Which will bring out the highlights in my eyes?'"

"You don't get it," Dillon says. "You are a walking fashion disaster, man. A federally declared state of emergency."

"Yeah," I add. "Do you wash that green T-shirt every night, or do you just own fifty of them?" I sniff the air. "Oh, my bad. You don't wash it at all."

The Wiffle ball bounces off my head.

Clothes matter. You dress like a loser, people will treat you like a loser. This is something Alex doesn't get. Alex spends his life staring at a computer screen and never looks in a mirror. I think it reflects well on me that I'm willing to be seen in the halls at school with somebody who looks like he might own a comb but can't remember where he put it on any given day.

Dillon, on the other hand, dresses right out of *GQ*. Dillon and I actually met over clothes. We'd had a couple of classes together, but we never hung out until last fall, when one day in English he leaned over and asked if I'd take Eileen Spence out on a date with him and Tamara Patterson. When I asked why me, he said, "Because you're the only guy in here I know who has a shirt without a Knicks logo on it."

Most of the time Dillon *won't* be seen in the halls with Alex. Dillon thinks hallway time is a serious socializing opportunity—and by socializing he doesn't mean hanging out with other guys. He's always at least three minutes late to class because he was talking—or something—with one of his girlfriends. He says he doesn't mind because detention is also prime girl-spotting turf.

I think the rumors about Dillon, the supply closet on the third floor, and the five-minute break between fourth and fifth periods are greatly exaggerated. I mean, some things are just physically impossible for a guy. In five minutes, anyway. When you count in the time to get up the stairs to the third floor and back down again in time for geometry.

"You're going to have to get some new clothes for that internship, right?" I ask Alex. "They won't let you into an office building in those sneakers." Alex's dog Fortran made an appetizer out of his left shoe last month. He just taped it up with duct tape.

"It's a programming internship. Everybody dresses like this. Geek is still in, didn't you notice?"

"Geek is only in if you have money like Bill Gates," I explain patiently. "Everywhere else it's still geek."

Dillon's phone rings. He waves at us to be quiet, checks to see who's calling, and puts the phone up to his ear.

"Hey, baby. What's up?"

Alex and I don't even try to look like we're not listening.

My room is so small there's no point anyway. The bed Dillon is sitting on takes up most of the space, and the rest of the floor is covered by the clothes I'm packing.

"Sure, I'm still coming over. Said I was, didn't I?"

Alex makes a nice bank shot into the trash can. Dillon kicks him on the shoulder and mouths, "Shut up!"

"Of course. You were worried? Hey, you don't have to worry about me. I'm leaving right now."

"Who was that?" I say as he switches off the phone.

"Emily."

"Emily who?" Alex asks. "Which one is Emily?"

"Emily, the blonde one. From algebra. You were in that class too, knucklehead. Remember, when Coltrane used to call her up to the board? The one with the legs?"

"The one who never got the differential equation?"

Dillon sighs heavily. "Since when does that matter in a girl? Didn't you hear me say about her legs?"

"You have to go?" I ask as I stuff socks inside my shoes.

"Nah."

"Didn't you tell her you were just leaving?"

"Sure."

It's hard for me to understand how Dillon gets away with this. I've dated a lot of girls and I even got pretty serious last year with Felicia Murray, before her dad got transferred and the whole family moved to Colorado. And in my experience, if I'm ten minutes late to a date I can kiss any action good-bye. Dillon can make them wait an hour and not even get a dirty look. My mom says if she catches me acting the way Dillon does around girls she'll ground me for a month to advance the cause of feminism. But when I asked her why the girls put up with it, she sighed and said it was one of the mysteries of the ages.

Dillon beats Alex hollow in twenty minutes of pro-level trash can basketball before he finally takes off to meet Emily.

"Do good work out there in the boonies," he says to me by way of good-bye. "Lots of hotties out there. Don't let them down."

"Don't worry," I say.

My mom catches him carefully combing his hair in the mirror beside the front door.

"It's a burden to be beautiful," she says.

"Ain't it the truth," Dillon says on his way out.

My mom rolls her eyes. She does that a lot around Dillon. Then she sticks her head into my room. "You staying for dinner?" she asks Alex.

When Alex walks in the door, my mom automatically adds extra spaghetti to the pot. Alex's mom says she can burn water. For most people this would be an exaggeration, but she *did* actually burn water once. Well, it wasn't really water. It was one of Alex's science experiments that she *thought* was water. She threw it over a pan of spontaneously combusting brownies. It wasn't a pretty sight. Or smell.

Alex shakes his head. "I have to meet my dad for dinner. We're going to his place for the weekend."

Alex's voice makes going to his dad's for the weekend sound about as appealing as a bout of hantavirus. My mom goes back to the kitchen and Alex keeps on talking.

"So he can tell me again how I ought to go out for a sport next fall, any sport, it doesn't matter, although of course soccer's the best. It'll look better on my college applications, you know." Right, because a GPA of 4.0 and 800 on the math SAT really won't impress the admissions officers that much. Alex whips the Wiffle ball so hard it ricochets off one wall and hits the opposite one. "Meanwhile, Rebecca will be trying to get him to notice her softball medal, and he'll say, 'That's nice, honey, but let me talk to your brother now,' and she'll go into the bathroom and cry."

I can't argue with his forecast, since, according to Alex anyway, this is exactly what happens whenever he and his little sister spend the weekend at his dad's.

"You could join the Ping-Pong team," I suggest. "And then remind him he said any sport would be okay."

"We don't have a Ping-Pong team at school."

"You could start one."

"Maybe I will."

"Anyway, it's only two days," I say, trying to be helpful.

"Two days plus Friday evening."

"But you come back on Sunday evening, so it still works out to two days."

"I guess."

"So," I say.

"Yeah."

"Right."

It's hard to believe I won't see Alex for a month. According to my mom, we became friends in first grade when I pushed him off the slide. I don't remember that. But since our moms are both single, they used to trade off babysitting, and we just got used to hanging out. Every summer since junior high, when our moms finally agreed we were too old for summer camp, we'd play computer games at his house, eat at mine, shoot some basketball down the street, or go to Central Park and watch the girls on Rollerblades glide by.

"Hey, you wouldn't have time to hang out this summer anyway," I say. "You're going to be protecting the free world. Writing software to catch the bad guys."

The computer firm Alex got the internship with does work for the Department of Defense. The idea of Alex being responsible for national security is truly scary. Half the time Alex can't remember where he left his glasses.

"Actually, I want to write the software that lets me spy on people's offshore bank accounts," he says.

"Also good."

Alex picks up his backpack.

"You're going to e-mail me, right?" he says. "Tell me all about . . ." He lowers his voice so my mom won't hear. "The mission. Regular reports."

I grin. "You got it. You'll have to live vicariously through me, since you won't see a girl all summer." I pretend to think for a minute. "On the other hand, that's nothing new."

He throws a punch at me. I dodge.

"You'll be back middle of July, huh?"

He knows this.

"Yeah."

"See ya."

"Yeah."

It feels weird, watching the door shut behind him. I go back to stuffing boxers and socks into what little space is left in my duffel bag.

"That's not really big enough for a month's worth of clothes," my mom says, coming over to look at what I'm doing. "You want to take my suitcase too?"

"Mom, your suitcase is pink."

"So?"

"So I think I'm going to have to deal with enough challenges to my masculinity as it is."

"Make sure you bring a jacket. It gets cold on the coast."

I point toward my jacket, lying on top of my backpack on the floor.

"It's beautiful out there," she goes on. "Your dad and I spent a weekend at Montauk just after we got married. We went walking by the water every morning."

I check to see if this is going to get weepy, but she's just smiling a little. My dad died when I was about three, in a car wreck. I don't remember him. But my mom still gets kind of misty-eyed when she brings him up. She goes out on a date or two every now and then, but nothing ever gets serious. I don't think she's met a guy yet who measures up to the way she remembers my dad.

Which is fine with me. The last thing I need is some new stepfather in my life, thinking he can tell me what to do.

"Did you remember your toothbrush?"

"No, I decided to opt out of dental hygiene. I thought it would be interesting to watch my teeth turn black and fall out."

"You're a lot less funny than you think. Did you know that?"

My genius is lost on these surroundings. I look up to see that my mom is holding something out to me. Something small and flat and rectangular and plastic.

"Don't look so excited," she says. "This is just for emergencies. I mean it. The bills will come to me, and if I see any charges for CDs or computer games or clothes . . . *especially* clothes, Justin . . ."

My mom doesn't actually have to finish her sentences when she's threatening me.

"I get it," I say, taking the credit card and stowing it away in my wallet. I have to admit I like the way it looks there, even if I'm not going to get to use it. "I'm not allowed to have any fun at all."

"Absolutely not," my mom says. "Okay, you're all set, looks like. Just remember . . ."

Why is she looking like that?

"I mean, the Beltons seem very nice and everything. It's just that they're . . ."

"Rich?" I say, to help her out.

"No, not rich. Just . . . well. Rich."

Let me put you in the picture here.

My mom: single parent, as described above. My dad, as I hear it, had a pretty good job with an accounting firm. My mom was in payroll there. She's still in payroll.

She makes decent money. We don't starve or anything. But her salary doesn't go far in New York. We live in a one-bedroom apartment with a sort of alcove off the living room where I sleep. Every year we cross our fingers that the rent doesn't go up too much. And we sure don't go on vacation to the Hamptons. Or for that matter, much of anywhere. Sometimes we go out to Jones Beach for the day or visit my Aunt Jill in New Jersey. But that's about it.

I'm not complaining. My mom does her best. I'm just saying we don't live like the Beltons.

"Don't worry," I reassure my mom. "I've got it all under control."

"Yeah?" She looks like she thinks I made a joke. "Well, I'm

relieved. Dinner in five minutes." She heads back into the kitchen. Then she yells.

"Justin! Bug duty!"

I pick up one of my shoes and follow her out into the kitchen. She points down on the floor, and I give the cockroach a good smack. I've been responsible for bug disposal since I was ten. My mom's pretty tough, but she doesn't like squashing cockroaches.

"Better call the exterminator while I'm away," I say, cleaning off the bottom of my shoe with a paper towel.

"Thanks, honey," she says. "What will I do without you?"

"Fall apart."

She snorts.

At least she doesn't look worried anymore. As if my ability to squash cockroaches guarantees me lifelong acceptance among the wealthy.

She stirs the spaghetti sauce. I go back to finish up my packing.

I wish I could tell my mom the truth. But I'm afraid it would hurt her feelings. She worked hard to bring me up. It's not her fault that she was left to do it on her own, or that my dad thought he was too young for life insurance.

But I'm not going to live like this all my life.

I've got plans. A's in high school, maybe a B+ or two. Scholarship to college. Law school. Corporate attorney. Maybe it won't be an apartment on Central Park West, not right away, anyway. But it sure won't be a one-bedroom dump in Queens, where the elevator breaks down once a week, where we get the exterminator in three times a year, and it still doesn't make much difference.

I want to tell my mom I'll do fine with the Beltons. With all the rich people and their summer beach houses. This is what it's going to be like in the future. This is more than just a summer job. It's even more than a mission to meet girls (which is not, however, unimportant).

It's a rehearsal for Justin Blakewell's Life, Act Two.

Chapter **4**

MAYBE I SHOULD EXPLAIN a little about the Hamptons.

The Hamptons are a string of towns along the coast of Long Island. East Hampton, Southampton, Bridgehampton, and a couple more that don't actually have "Hampton" in the name but still count. Some people live there year-round, but mostly New Yorkers come out to spend the summers. It's supposed to look like small-town America. Main Street with trees and baskets of flowers hanging from the lampposts.

It's nothing like Manhattan. I guess that's the point. Rich people like to have a break sometimes from their Central Park West condos and Upper East Side penthouses. So they come out here and pretend they live in the country. Only it's country without cows or cornfields or right-wing militias. Country with a few celebrities down the street and a Tiffany's next to the Starbucks.

Really. I saw it when we drove in.

Personally, I think when I get rich I'll have a penthouse so nice I'll *never* get tired of it. But it's all according to taste.

"At last," Mr. Belton says as he pulls up the car in the driveway.

What a minute. Where's the beach? Where are all the girls in bikinis?

"About two blocks that way," Mr. Belton says when I ask (about the beach, not about the girls). "Take this into the cottage, would you, Justin?"

This is not what I would call a cottage, I think, as I drag a massive suitcase into the front hall. A cottage is something *small*. This is not small. This has got a living room with a big-screen TV. A den with an electronic setup that even Alex would approve of. A master bedroom, a room for Aspen, a room for me, and one left over for Steven Spielberg in case he shows up and wants to stay the night.

Not bad at all.

Mr. Belton's dragging stuff in from the car. Mrs. Belton's opening drawers and cabinets in the kitchen, as if she thinks a burglar might have broken in and left some canned goods. She told me to call her Gayle on the way up, but I'm having a little trouble with that, so mostly I'm calling her "Ummm." As in, "Ummm. Should I take Aspen to the can, I mean, the restroom?"

I like her, though, at least better than I thought I was going to after that interview. She talks really fast, but most of the time she doesn't actually expect you to answer, so it's pretty easy being around her. Not like some adults, who seem to think that because they've got some years on you they have the right to interrogate you. How do you like school? What's your favorite class? Thinking of going to college? Hey, do I ask about *your* personal life? So how's the dead-end job? Getting along with the wife? Planning on doing something about that bald spot?

Anyway, Mrs. Belton doesn't do that. And she doesn't have

a bad figure for an older woman either. Blonde hair, nice haircut, the kind my mom says she wants but never gets because she always goes to the same place that only cuts hair one way, fifteen bucks, no blow-dry.

I don't have much of a feel yet for Mr. Belton. He didn't say a lot on the ride up, except to sing along to some hits of the '70s. And I guess you can't really blame a guy for the decade he grew up in.

Aspen's running in a big circle around the living room. I guess he sat still for too long in the car.

"Aspen! Stop!" his mom yells. He stops running and starts jumping up and down instead.

"Justin, please, can you take the knee-high terror outside?" Mrs. Belton asks. "There's a park down the street. Let him run off some of that energy."

"Sure," I say. Okay with me. Gets me out of unloading the car.

"Thanks, Justin," Mrs. Belton says. "Honey? Did we buy this? Do you remember buying this?" She's holding up a can of chicken livers.

Time to leave.

Aspen and I walk down the block. I'd kind of pictured the Hamptons as one long strip of sand with water on one side and mansions on the other, but I guess it's a little more complicated than that. This is just block after block of houses, wide lawns, and more trees than I've seen anywhere outside of Central Park.

At the first intersection, I step off the curb to cross the street and realize that Aspen's not with me. He's standing still with both feet on the sidewalk.

"What's up, buddy?" I ask.

He says something, a breathy little whisper. I lean down to hear better.

"I can't cross the street by myself." That's what he says.

"You're not *by* yourself," I point out. "I'm right here."

"You have to hold my hand." Again, I have to bend over to hear him. Who made kids so short?

I look up and down the street. I haven't seen another car since we got here. It's so quiet, it sounds to me like there might never be another car again. But who am I to argue with the rules? I offer Aspen my hand. He takes it. His is warm and damp, but he has some strength to that grip. I can see him now, a corporate CEO, intimidating the competition with his power handshake. Of course, they'll be less intimidated when they find out he's not allowed to cross the street alone.

He doesn't let go of my hand all the way to the park.

Once we're there, though, he knows exactly what he wants to do. He heads straight for the slide. Up the ladder, moving one hand, then a foot, then the other hand, then the other foot. Slower than a dial-up modem. Once he's at the top, he slides down, runs back, and does it again.

Fine. Everything under control. I take a look around the park for the real objective of this mission.

Houston, we have a problem

There are kids a-plenty, just like I imagined. Swinging, sliding, climbing, kicking balls, digging, screaming. Man, how do little kids hit that particular pitch? It's like nails on a blackboard. I can feel it go in my ears and all the way down my spine. They should try playing tapes of this at terrorists they're trying to get to confess.

Plenty of kids. Plenty of nannies too. All according to plan. Except for one thing.

These nannies are girls, all right. But they're *old* girls. I mean, women. I mean, not really datable material. Most of them are sitting on benches, occasionally yelling out "Don't!" and "Stop!" and "You get over here!" which the kids are pretty much ignoring.

The manny mission is not going according to plan. Do I have the wrong park? Are all the young, thin, unwrinkled nannies somewhere else?

Hey—wait a minute.

She's standing by the sandbox. She's got on cropped pants and a T-shirt that makes me thank the CEOs of Banana Republic, the Gap, and every other chain store that decided the look for summer was tight and clingy. Long, thick dark hair with just a little curl to it. She has her back to me. Does the front live up to the back? Don't let this be a disappointment, please.

Aspen's still going up and down the slide, regular as clockwork. I drift away a few steps. Casual. I wish I smoked. That would give me a good excuse to stand here doing nothing. Right now I'm just stuck in the middle of a playground, hands in my pockets, trying to look like I'm not staring at—

Ah. She turns around.

It's not a disappointment.

Can't be caught looking. I glance over at Aspen, just in time to see a bigger kid grab him by the back of his shirt and pull him away from the ladder. Oops. Sorry, vision of loveliness. Duty calls. Don't go away.

The big kid, who looks to be about six, with hair as orange

as a carrot, goes down the slide headfirst. I look around to see who's watching him, but nobody seems particularly interested. Aspen's hanging back uncertainly near the ladder. The redheaded kid runs around again, pushes by Aspen, and starts to climb up.

"Hey," I say. "I think this kid was waiting for a turn."

Calm. Reasonable. Authoritative. All those things.

The kid ignores me. Runs up the ladder before I can grab him. And Aspen's looking at me like I'm supposed to fix this. Well, I will.

When the redheaded kid hits the bottom of the slide, I'm standing there. Looking down at him. Tough.

"You've got to wait your turn," I say.

"No, I don't," the kid says.

"Yes, you do," I'm about to say back, when it strikes me as undignified to argue with a six-year-old. Instead, I lean over and look him in the eye.

I make a little suggestion. Then I smile. Widen my eyes a bit. Just a touch of Jack Nicholson in *The Shining*. Don't want to overdo it.

The kid doesn't believe me. But he doesn't quite not believe me either. He backs up a few steps and runs toward the swings.

"What did you *do* to that kid?" says a voice behind me.

I turn around.

Well, it's not one of the old nannies. But it's not the vision of loveliness either. She looks to be about my age. Her jeans are ripped on one knee. Her T-shirt is baggy, not that it looks like there'd be much to cling to even if she had heeded the call of Banana Republic, the Gap, etc. Her hair isn't a bad color, blonde with lots of light streaks that somehow look like they came from the sun and not a salon. But it's pulled back in a tight ponytail with bits sticking out. It's a style that does nothing for her skinny face.

I shrug. "Go ahead. You can go on the slide now," I say to Aspen.

He shakes his head.

"No, really. That mean kid's gone. Go on, slide."

Aspen points toward the sandbox.

"You're done sliding?" I ask in disbelief.

He nods.

"Fine." I roll my eyes. My Oscar-worthy tribute to Jack was wasted. "Go to the sandbox. Whatever."

The skinny girl's still looking at me. Like she's waiting for an answer.

"He was pushing my kid around," I say. "I just told him to quit."

"Yeah, but how'd you make him?" she asks. "That's Bryson. He's a real bully. His nanny never does a thing about it."

She actually sounds impressed. Not pissed.

"Told him I was a kidnapper," I say. "Looking for kids who don't wait their turn."

"Ah," she says. "Terrifying defenseless small children. Playing on their deepest fears."

"Damn straight," I say.

She grins. "I like it."

Her name's Liz. She's watching Max, a grubby little kid playing in the sandbox who looks to be about the same age as Aspen. Max has sand under his fingernails, all over his shirt, and even up his nose, but it doesn't seem to bother him, or Liz.

I follow Liz back to the sandbox, naturally, since a glance shows me that the girl in the tight T-shirt is still there. "C'mon, Max." Now Liz is on her knees in the sand. "Let's build a big ramp here. Then your truck can drive on it. Hey, what's your name, Aspen? You want to help?"

They're all burrowing in the sand like prairie dogs. I look over at the objective of the manny mission. Smile a little. Not looking too eager. She looks back, no smile, but not displeased either.

"Hey, Serafina, come on and dig." Liz looks up at the mission objective. Now I know her name and I didn't even have to ask.

"No, thank you. I just did my nails." She spreads her fingers out so her nails sparkle in the sun. Red like pomegranate seeds.

"Fina did my nails too," pipes up a little voice. This must be the kid Serafina's watching. A little girl, maybe three or so, with curly red hair in a ponytail right on top of her head, like a fountain spouting water. She holds out her fingers seriously for Liz's inspection. Each nail is a different color. Blue, purple, lime green, orange, pink. Serafina smiles and shrugs a little. It's charming.

"Very pretty, Molly," Liz says gravely.

"Sophisticated," I say. "I sense a new fashion trend." I try my best grin on Serafina. "I'm Justin."

She doesn't smile back. But she does look at me. "Hello," she says.

Is there a nicer word in the English language?

ASPEN'S IN BED. I'm watching some old movie in the living room with the Beltons. I've decided, at least in my own head, to call them Mr. and Mrs. B. It's easier than "Kevin" and "Gayle" and a lot more cool than "Ummm."

Gotta love the big-screen TV. It even has a cupboard all to itself in the wall, so when it's closed you'd never know there's anything there. But open it up and it's high-definition city. The movie they've got on, though, some old black-and-white thing, is pretty much a waste of all this technology. And the Beltons are curled up together on the cough, getting a little more cuddly than I care to stick around and witness. I clear my throat. "Is it okay if I use the computer?"

"Sure." Mr. B waves the hand that his wife doesn't have a hold of. "You don't have to ask, Justin. Do whatever you want."

I make a quick and strategic retreat into the den. Who knew that married people even carried on like that? I thought that once you had a kid or two, the hormones sort of calmed down. Apparently not.

I wonder if *my* mom and dad . . .

This is not a train of thought I want to pursue any further. There's a little laptop perched on the desk in the den. The thing's hardly thicker than my brand-new credit card, but I bet it's got twice the RAM of the old clunkers they have at my school. Wireless Internet access, of course. Sweet. I log on and open up a new e-mail.

To: alxskywlkr@webmail.com
To: playboy311@netwave.com
From: justinb597@webmail.com
Subject: Manny Mission Report #1

Mission objective spotted! Code name: Serafina. 5'5", perhaps 126 lbs, brunette. Meets all specifications. First contact established. Will proceed to next stage. Further reports to follow.

I hit SEND and then open up the e-mail my mom wrote me from work.

To: justinb597@webmail.com
From: Lblakewell@walkerandco.com
Subject: Hello!

Honey—
The apartment seems so quiet without you. Hmmm. Maybe that's a good thing! Hope you are settling in. Tell me what it's like. Started work for my new boss today. Seems like a Barney, but we'll see. Can't write more, he's coming this direction!
Love,
Mom

Since Mom can only e-mail from her work account, we've developed a code based on Saturday morning cartoons. A Barney is Barney Rubble—it means a decent type but not too bright. That's not bad in a boss. The last one she had was a Marvin, as in Marvin the Martian. A total loony on a power trip. Of course he got promoted. That kind always do, Mom says.

I hit REPLY.

To: Lblakewell@walkeranco.com
From: justinb597@webmail.com
Subject: Re: Hello

You should see this place. I think the bathroom is bigger than our whole apartment! (Just joking.) But it's really cool. I've got my own room with a phone and a CD player and everything. I took Aspen to the park and met a couple of

I stop typing and hit DELETE several times.

and didn't lose him or break him or anything.

Then I take out the part about the CD player too. I don't want to make it sound like this place is better than home.

This is turning out to be a pretty short e-mail. After a while I give up, type "More later!" and hit SEND.

There's not much else to do except go back to my room and unpack, unless I want to return to the living room and watch a movie where nothing gets blown up. It doesn't take long to put my clothes away. The closet seems to swallow up the three shirts and two pairs of pants I hang up in it. My jeans, shorts, T-shirts, boxers, and bathing suit take up two drawers in the dresser. And that's about it.

I pop a CD into the player and stretch out on the bed. Funny to be in a bedroom where the bed doesn't take up most of the floor space. I spend the rest of the evening planning the smooth and suave things I will say to Serafina when I meet her again.

In the morning I lie still for a while with my eyes closed, wondering what happened to all the traffic. And what is that racket that sounds like a warped CD right outside my window?

Then I open my eyes. Oh yeah, I'm in the Hamptons. And the noise is coming from a bunch of birds in a tree close to the house.

And people say the city is loud.

I roll over and look at the clock. Mrs. Belton said last night they'd have breakfast at eight o'clock. Eight in the morning in the summer. On a *Sunday* in the summer. Cruel and unusual doesn't even begin to cover it.

Well, I guess if it was fun nobody would call it work.

It's 7:40 now. I get up, drag a T-shirt on over my boxers, bounce off the doorframe, and ricochet out into the hallway. Mornings are not my best time.

"Good morning, Justin!"

Who is this cheerful at the crack of dawn? Oh, right. Mrs. Belton. It's kind of weird, seeing her. I'm used to meeting my mom on my way to the bathroom in the morning, but that's, you know, my mom. Mrs. B is, well, not my mom. She's younger, for one thing. And my mom wears a T-shirt and sweatpants to bed, but Mrs. B's wearing a dark blue silky robe, holding it closed with one hand at the neck. Her feet are bare. Before I can stop it, my brain is suddenly speculating about what *else* is bare.

Stop it. Stop it now. *Right now.*

"Breakfast in about twenty minutes, okay?" she says.

I mean to say "Uh-huh." Or "Sure." Or "Sounds great." What actually comes out of my mouth is more like "Uh—hurgh." I'm absolutely refusing to let my eyes go anywhere other than her chin.

"See you downstairs," she says, and disappears back into her bedroom.

I hope a quick shower will help clear my head of things that definitely should not be in there.

Mr. and Mrs. B have their own bathroom off their bedroom. Aspen and I are sharing the one in the hall. Which means that there's a bunch of plastic toys in the bathtub, left over from Aspen's bath last night. I've forgotten about this until my foot comes down hard on a little plastic fish with a sharp, pointy fin.

I yell. I hop around a little bit. Hopping is not the best idea in a bathtub. At least, when I fall over, I manage to end up sitting on the toilet. Thank goodness the lid's down.

There's a knock at the door.

"Justin? Is everything okay?"

It's Mrs. B. She sounds worried.

Oh great. Not only have I shown her that I can't speak in the mornings, but I've also just proven that I can't go to the bathroom by myself.

"Fine!" I say brightly, like yelling and falling over in the bathtub are just part of my prebreakfast exercise routine.

"All right, then," Mrs. B says, a bit doubtfully.

I wish the shower could wash away my short-term memory. But at least it wakes me up a little. And brushing my teeth helps too, although the only toothpaste the Beltons have is some funky baking powder stuff. My teeth may be clean, but my mouth tastes like something you'd use to scrub out the fridge.

I make it down to the kitchen by 7:58, but nobody's there. A pot of coffee is bubbling away on the counter and a box of healthy-looking cereal is sitting next to it. I pour myself a cup of coffee and slice a banana into a bowl of the thick brown flakes. Baking soda toothpaste and now shredded tree bark breakfast food. When I'm rich, I'm going to eat stuff for breakfast that actually tastes good.

Then I try to figure out where everybody has gone.

Finally I get it. They're sitting around the table on the back deck. I guess eating outside is something rich people do.

It's *bright* out on the deck. All this sunlight and blue sky and fresh air is too much so early in the morning.

The Beltons are reading the paper. Aspen is sitting by the stairs that lead from the deck down into the backyard, digging in the dirt with a stick.

I say hi. They say good morning. Mr. B lifts one eyebrow as he watches me put sugar in my coffee.

"You don't *have* to drink coffee, you know," he says, watching me dump the fifth spoonful in and stir.

"I like coffee," I say. Well, I do. If it's sweet enough.

All of a sudden there's a burst of noise coming from next door. It's almost like machine-gun fire, if machine-gun fire were real high pitched.

"Oh, great," Mr. B says, flipping over a page of the paper. "Yippy and Yappy are back."

"Who?" I ask.

"The dogs. Next door. Obnoxious little things."

"They're very friendly," Mrs. B says.

He grunts.

I look over, but there's a wooden fence between the Beltons and their neighbors, so I can't see the dogs. I can only hear them. It's hard to believe there's just two of them.

I swallow a big bite of the healthy cereal and realize that Aspen is standing at my elbow.

I nearly choke. The kid's like a secret agent. Belton, Aspen Belton. Licensed to startle. Aspen has his hands out in front of him, cupped into a hollow around something.

"Look," he whispers. His voice practically vibrates with excitement.

He opens his hands very carefully.

He's holding a bug.

Not a cockroach or anything slimy. A pill bug. A roly-poly, I used to call them when I was a kid. You touch them, and they curl up into a perfectly round little ball.

"You hold it, you hold it." Aspen tips the bug into my hand. He waits for it to uncurl and then pokes it. It curls up. Aspen giggles like a miniature mad scientist.

"That's so cool. Isn't that so cool, Justin?"

And he really wants me to say how cool it is. I can see it actually matters, like I have the ultimate vote on coolness. He's found this bug that he thinks is the greatest thing since the Hope diamond, but it won't be really cool unless I say so.

So I do.

"Yeah, that's really cool, Aspen."

"I found it. In the dirt."

"Yeah, I know." Something more seems to be called for. "I mean, great job. You think there are any more?"

"More?"

It seems impossible, but his eyes get even wider than before. Then he runs back down the steps to keep on digging in the dirt.

I catch Mrs. B smiling at me over her coffee cup.

"Justin," she says as I sit there with a pill bug in my hand. "We've got to go shopping this morning. How about taking Aspen to the beach?"

"Sure," I answer, trying to sound casual. Actually, I'm pretty excited. At last, it's time for the beach, the girls in bathing suits, and the true Hamptons experience. Meanwhile, I'm wondering what to do with the pill bug. I would just put it down on the deck, but will Aspen be upset if I lose it? Am I supposed to eat cereal with one hand and hold the bug with the other?

"Just drop it," says Mr. B. "He'll never remember he gave it to you."

I set the little bug free to resume its buggy life down under the deck.

After breakfast, Mr. B collects the dishes, and Mrs. B starts tossing stuff into an ugly baby blue shoulder bag for me to take to the beach. The thing is, though, Aspen's only four years old. How much stuff can a person that small actually need?

"Water," she says. "Juice box. Animal crackers. Plastic ball. Shovel. Sunscreen. Towels. Here's a clean pair of shorts, in case, you know."

I know what?

Oh.

"Band-Aids. He likes the ones with the smiley faces on them. Cell phone. Do you know how to use this kind?"

I nod.

"Here's some change anyway. And our cell number, I'll keep the other phone with us. And our pediatrician. And emergency."

She actually thinks I don't know 911.

"Can you think of anything else?"

I shake my head.

"Okay, then."

Mr. B's waiting in the car for her, and they take off. Before I collect Aspen from the backyard, I dump all the stuff out of the blue shoulder bag and put it in my backpack, which is plain black. I may be a manny, but that doesn't mean I have to look stupid doing it.

Chapter 6

EVEN THOUGH MR. B told me that the cottage is only two blocks from the beach, it turns out that's not where I'm supposed to take Aspen. To get to the main beach, with the lifeguard and everything, you have to go back into town, down Main Street. Mrs. B said a bike is the easiest way to get there.

So I get Mr. B's bike out of the garage. I'm about to boost Aspen up into the kiddie seat when he squeals, "Look!" then squirms out of my hands, and hits the ground at full speed.

I grab for him, thinking he's about to run out into the street, but it turns out that he's only headed next door, where Yippy and Yappy are going out for their morning walk.

My first reaction is surprise that dogs so little could make so much noise. They don't really look like dogs at all, actually. More like little white wigs with feet. One of them's got a pink bow holding its hair away from its eyes.

By the time I get over there, Aspen is on his knees, being jumped on and getting his face licked and generally having a great time. I grab hold of the dogs' double leash and try to untangle it from the legs of the woman taking them out. She's twisting around and gasping, "No—oh dear—my goodness—please—"

"Sorry," I say. "He likes dogs."

She's got herself unwound now and pulls the dogs away from Aspen. I'm about at the level of her knees, and I notice that her sneakers are dyed the same light purple as her yoga pants.

"Oh dear," she says again, pulling on the leash. "Oh no, I'm sorry. Please don't pet them. They've just been groomed."

I guess that means somebody actually *wanted* them to look this way. Go figure.

"We don't like to let strangers pet them," she explains to me in this high, breathy voice. "They could pick up an infection, you know."

The dogs are yipping and standing on their hind legs, leaning against the leash, trying to get back to Aspen and get petted some more. And the grin is melting off Aspen's face.

I don't see what harm it could do to let the kid pet the dogs. It's not like he's sick or something. She makes it sound like he's crawling with germs.

"Sorry," I say, and get Aspen by the hand and haul him to his feet. "He didn't mean any harm."

Aspen's lower lip is starting to turn down in a pout.

"Oh, I know," the neighbor lady gushes. "It's just, we can't be too careful, you know? Good-bye, good morning." And she power walks off down the street with the dogs yapping around her heels.

I look down at Aspen. The pout is reaching catastrophic proportions.

"Hey, buddy, don't worry," I say. "Maybe there'll be some dogs at the beach you can pet. *Better* dogs." I say that last part loud enough, I hope, for the neighbor lady to hear.

Aspen sighs heavily, like the world is a difficult and unreasonable place. But he hangs on to my hand and lets me lead him back to the bike.

Before she left, Mrs. B also told me I have to wear a helmet when I've got Aspen out on the bike. Now, a sleek, aerodynamic, jet-black bicycle helmet isn't the worst fashion accessory in the world. But this one is clunky, thick, and bright yellow. I'm going to look like a Chiquita banana.

Aspen has a matching one. Great. Now we'll be a pair of Chiquita bananas.

I hoist Aspen up into the kiddie seat and buckle his helmet under his chin. Then I look around carefully. The Beltons are already gone. So nobody's going to know if I skip the helmet thing, right?

But the dog-walking lady isn't too far away. And there could be other neighbors watching, neighbors who might just mention to the Beltons that their new manny was seen on a bike without protective headgear. I jam the helmet on and jump on the bike. Let's get this over with as quickly as possible.

After a few blocks I start thinking that Lance Armstrong should train with a four-year-old in the kiddie seat and he'd chew up the Tour de France. I mean, well, more than he does already. I'm breathing pretty hard by the time we swing onto Main Street. Great. Now I'm a panting, out-of-shape Chiquita banana.

"Faster!" Aspen shouts just as we're pulling up even with a bunch of girls in bikini tops and shorts. They look amused. Believe me, kid, I'm going as fast as I can. I want to get this over with as quickly as possible. I stand up on the pedals to get some more speed. We rocket along under baskets of flowers hanging from the lampposts. Does somebody come along with a ladder to water them every night? Or maybe a watering can on a really long pole? We zoom past a pricey-looking restaurant, with tin tubs of bushy green plants on the steps and the name ANTONIO'S in swirly type over the doors. A coffee place. A bookstore. Then Main Street swoops into a big curve and there's a sign for the beach.

We spin off into a parking lot with a place called Jack's Shack selling hot dogs and ice cream. First thing I do is pull off the yellow helmet and run my hands through my hair before it melds to my skull. Then I unbuckle Aspen and lift him down. He takes off at a run for the water, and I have to yell at him to wait while I lock up the bike.

Once I catch up with Aspen, he heads straight down the beach for an old dock where all the kids seem to be playing. Then he starts a game with the waves, getting near enough to let them nibble his toes and running back, shrieking. When I get my feet in the water I don't blame him. It's *cold*. Turn-your-toenails-blue cold. Man, if I ever do get tired of my penthouse, I think I'll have a beach house in Florida. The Virgin Islands. Hawaii.

While Aspen's occupied, I take a look around at the scenery. Girls in tank tops, girls in bikinis. Not bad. Not bad at all.

"Okay. Watch out. Out of the way, everybody! Here goes!"

The voice sounds familiar. I look up to see Liz standing on

the dock, waving little kids out of the way. I confess she doesn't look as bad in a bathing suit as I would have thought. But she's still not in Serafina's class.

She backs up a few steps. Then she runs down the length of the dock and leaps into the air, cannonballing into the water. All the little kids go wild. I notice Max clapping his hands and yelling. She splashes them and then swims back alongside the dock to the shore.

"I cannot believe you did that," I say when she gets there.

"Oh, hi." She squeezes water out of her ponytail. "It's Justin, right? From the park yesterday."

"How cold is that water?" She has goose bumps all over.

"Not that bad. Invigorating. You should try it."

"No way." I shake my head. "You've frozen some brain cells or something. That's not swimming water."

"Coward." She looks over at Aspen. "Hey, Aspen, you want to see Justin jump off the dock, right?"

Aspen nods eagerly.

"Tough," I say. "You can't always get what you want."

"What a wimp," Liz sneers, looking me up and down. But I'm strong. I don't need to prove my manhood. I am not going to be blackmailed into swimming in the deep freeze.

"Yes, very wimpy," says another voice behind my back.

Damn.

The sight of Serafina in a light pink bathing suit pretty much seizes up my vocal cords, not to mention a few other parts of my anatomy. Suddenly a dip in icy cold water doesn't seem like such a bad idea. I climb up on the dock.

Liz starts the chant. Soon the kids pick it up. "Jus-TIN! Jus-TIN! Jus-TIN!"

I hold up my hands to acknowledge my audience. The little people, how they love me. I bow.

Liz changes the chant.

"Stall-ING! Stall-ING!"

I take off down the dock. Old splintery wood under my feet. Nice warm sunlight on my arms and back and chest. I get to the end of the dock and don't give myself enough time to think before I jump.

I feel myself in the air for a split second, like I'm floating, not falling.

Why am I doing this again?

I thought it was cold back at the edge, when I was just dipping my feet in. This water clearly just melted off the Arctic ice shelf. My blood is rapidly congealing in my veins.

"Hey, Justin. You okay?"

Liz is kneeling on the edge of the dock, looking down at me as I tread water. She seems slightly concerned.

I give her a dirty look and start swimming back toward shore.

"Guess we should have warned you," she calls after me. "It's a little cold."

"Do it again!" Aspen says when I'm out of the water and rubbing every inch of my skin hard with a towel.

"No way," I say, remembering in time not to add "in hell."

"Again!"

"*You* do it again!" I growl, dropping the towel to chase him. "I'm going to catch you!" I roar. "And throw you in! And make you swim home!"

He's laughing so much he can barely run, so I don't chase him very hard. Somehow I end up chasing Max and Molly too, up and down the beach, until we're all worn out and drop down on our towels to rest.

Liz and Serafina have spread their towels out next to mine. The manny mission is progressing nicely.

Information gathered by the time we're ready to leave the beach:

Serafina is originally from Buenos Aires. But her family moved here when she was five. She still speaks Spanish at home with her mother and when they go back to visit.

She lives in Manhattan now. But her family comes to the Hamptons every summer. That's how she knows Liz, who's local. "So how long have you known each other?" I ask Serafina, looking over at Liz too. Showing an interest. Asking questions. Very important for the achievement of the mission. Aspen, Max, and Molly are all busy digging a hole in the sand big enough to climb into, so I can concentrate on making Serafina think I'm charming.

"Oh, we met three years ago. Isn't that right, Liz? At the beach," Serafina says. "Liz was babysitting for her sisters."

Liz snorts. She's not nearly as elegant as Serafina. "That's not what happened," she says.

"Yes, it is. We met at the beach. That's not wrong."

"We didn't just 'meet,'" Liz objects. "I was flying a kite for Annie and Ellie—they're my little sisters—and I was running backward, you know, looking up at the kite, and I tripped over Fina and gave her a bloody nose."

"See?" Serafina says. "We met at the beach."

"And how'd you get this job?" I ask, continuing to display my interest.

"My father thought I should take a summer job, for the experience," she explains. Not for the money, I note. If knowing that she lives in Manhattan and summers in the Hamptons wasn't a big enough clue that she's rich, this would be another tip-off. "My parents have gone back to Argentina this month, but I wanted to come here. So this way I can live with Molly's family and still see my friends."

"Fina got me the job with Max's family," Liz adds. "They know Molly's parents, and they were looking for a nanny."

"So, what about you, Justin?" Serafina asks. "There are not so many boys who are nannies."

Perfect opportunity to trot out the Mr. Sensitive line. I'm about to get started when we hear a car horn blasting from the parking lot behind us. Liz jumps up and starts stuffing Max's belongings into her bag.

"He's early. Max! Come on, we have to leave!"

"I'll pack," Serafina says quickly. "You get him ready."

Max doesn't want to leave yet. The hole's only half-dug. But Liz has the sand brushed off him and a shirt over his head before he has time to start whining. Serafina follows them up the beach with the bag. For some reason I follow behind Serafina, like I'm on a string. So we all get to see Max's dad chew Liz out.

"I said quarter to eleven, Liz. Don't you have a watch? I don't have time to waste."

Perfectly pressed chinos, shirt and tie, sunglasses. He must go to the same hairdresser as Mrs. B. I really don't like him.

"You said quarter after, Mr. McGraw," Liz answers him, her voice real quiet, but firm.

"Quarter *to*!" he snaps. "Go on, get in. Max, hurry up."

Nice affectionate greeting for his son.

Liz doesn't say another word. She helps Max into the car seat in the back of the shiny blue SUV and climbs in after him. Mc-Graw gives Serafina and me a look like it's our fault too and gets into the driver's seat. I see Liz's head snap back as he takes off.

"He did say quarter after," Serafina says quietly. "I heard him."

She could have said that to his face, I think. But it probably wouldn't have done any good. It's obviously not in Mr. McGraw's universe that a teenager could be right and he could be wrong.

This should be the perfect time to make some real progress on the manny mission, since it's just Serafina and me and the two little kids. But watching Liz with Max's dad makes everything feel awkward. Not exactly the moment for romance.

"I should probably get Molly home," Serafina says.

"Uh-huh," I answer with breathtaking intelligence, and we head back to our towels so she can pack up Molly's stuff. Molly's about two-thirds the size of Aspen, but she's got three times as much gear. Go figure.

"So, uh," I say as Serafina packs sunscreen and a fuzzy pink rabbit away in a bag. "Maybe . . ."

"Yes?" Serafina asks.

And I lose my nerve. Completely.

There she is, looking at me with those dark eyes, little wisps of her hair blowing in the wind, waiting for me to finish my sentence. And all that comes out of my mouth is the lamest good-bye line in history.

"Maybe I'll see you around. I guess."

She nods. Finishes packing. Makes Molly wave good-bye to

Aspen. Leaves me sitting there with a little kid and a half-dug hole.

"Maybe I could call you sometime," I mutter at Aspen. Six words. Only two of them are longer than one syllable. Why should six little words be so hard to say?

Chapter 7

I'VE NEVER SEEN PEOPLE SHOP like the Beltons shop. By the time I get Aspen back from the beach, they've already got one load of groceries in the house, but apparently that's not enough. The spend the rest of the day doing errands. We could cross Alaska by dogsled with all the supplies they're laying in.

Late in the afternoon, I'm in the kitchen with my head in the fridge, getting something for Aspen to drink. I spot the apple juice, but while I'm at it I check out the other offerings. Beer . . . well, probably not, not while I'm on duty, so to speak. Orange juice, white wine, Diet Coke . . . okay, there's the real stuff, actual Coke with sugar in it. Let's go wild. I've got the apple juice on one hand and a can of Coke in the other when the kitchen door opens behind me. I jump like I've been caught with my hand in Mr. B's wallet and stuff the Coke back on the shelf behind the OJ. I swear, I don't have a clue why. I mean, nobody said it wasn't okay for me to have a Coke if I want. Then again, nobody said it was.

Anyway. I pour some juice for Aspen as Mr. B comes in

carrying a bag made of green nylon string and full of something smelly. Mrs. B follows him with a flat square package wrapped in brown paper, holding it in both hands like it's fragile.

"Typical," Mr. B says, dumping the bag in the sink. "We go out for groceries and *I* end up doing the shopping while *she* checks out the galleries."

"Typical," Aspen agrees, bobbing his head up and down. I hand him a glass of apple juice. His dad fills a huge pot with water and sets it to boil on the stove while he gets the rest of the groceries and puts them away.

Meanwhile, Mrs. B lays the package flat on the counter, well away from Aspen and his juice, gets a pair of scissors, and starts cutting the paper off. I get myself some water— there can't be anything wrong with water, right?—and lean against the fridge to watch as she peels away the wrapping. "There." She sighs. "Isn't that beautiful?"

Ummm . . .

"Gorgeous," Mr. B says seriously. "Right, Justin?"

"Oh, yeah," I agree, straight-faced. "Absolutely. Right, Aspen?"

"Ab-slootly," Aspen echoes me.

"Philistines!" Mrs. B throws up her hands. "I am surrounded by barbarians. Jackson Pollock got his start in the Hamptons, you know. He paid a grocery bill with a painting that's worth about a million dollars today. This could be just the same. Let's see where we're going to hang it."

She waltzes out of the kitchen with the painting in her hands. This painting, by the way, pretty much looks like an exploding eggplant to me.

"Honey?" Mrs. B calls. You can see into the living room from the kitchen, over the counter where Aspen's sitting with his juice, so we can watch her hold the artwork up to one wall and then another. "How about right here?"

"That's great, dear."

"You're not even looking!"

"I'm getting dinner ready. I trust you." Mr. B picks up the scissors and starts cutting open the bag that's in the sink. That's when I notice that the bag is moving.

"What's *that?*"

"Dinner," Mr. B says. "Freshest lobster you've ever tasted."

I refrain from mentioning that it'll be the *only* lobster I've ever tasted. Fresh is certainly right, though. These lobsters are so fresh they're still alive. They're crawling around, trying feebly and stupidly to get out of the sink. Their claws are taped up so they can't cut their way to freedom. It's lobster Alcatraz.

"I thought lobsters were red," I say. These are kind of mottled green and brown. "Do they have to get ripe or something?"

I hear Mrs. B laughing from the living room. She thinks I'm making a joke.

"They turn red when you cook them," Mr. B explains.

"Hey, this one's mine." Very carefully, I reach in and pick one up. It sure doesn't look or smell like something I'd want to eat. Its claws wave and its little legs scrabble in the air. "I'm going to name it . . . Lobzilla. Here, Aspen, this one's yours." I pick up another one. "Grr! Aarrrrgh!" Lobzilla and Aspen's dinner have a mock battle in the middle of the kitchen. "What're you going to name yours?"

"Barney," Aspen says.

First thing I'm going to have to do is change this kid's TV-watching habits. On the other hand, I kind of like the idea of Lobzilla tackling Barney. Who will emerge triumphant? The lobsters battle back and forth across the kitchen. Aspen cheers as Barney knocks Lobzilla flat on his back and then does a little lobster dance over his body.

"Okay, Justin, toss them in." Mr. B takes the lid off the pot on the stove. Steam whooshes out. The water inside bubbles.

"What? In there?"

"Sure."

"Aren't we going to . . . kill them first?"

"They'll die pretty quick in the water," Mr. B says. "Here, you want me to do it?"

I certainly do. These Wall Street types really are ruthless. I hand over Lobzilla and Barney and quickly head out of the kitchen so I don't have to watch the lid go back on the pot. That's it. I'm never eating anything again that doesn't come wrapped up in plastic on a Styrofoam tray.

About half an hour later, Lobzilla is bright red and sitting on my plate. His long lobster feelers lie limply across the china. His little lobster eyes are looking up at me.

Mrs. B is cracking open Aspen's lobster for him. Rip off the claws. Pull off the legs. Okay. I can do this. This is how rich people eat. I'm going to have to learn sometime.

I break open a claw and tug out a steaming chunk of meat. Imitating Mr. B, I dunk it in a little pot of melted butter.

Oh, man.

Sorry, Lobzilla, but that tastes *good*.

"See? It's worth it," Mr. B says, wiping butter off his chin.

I can't argue.

After dinner, I teach Aspen to play War. Every time he flips over a card that's higher than mine, he squeals. I'm surprised the glasses in the kitchen don't shatter.

Mrs. B yawns. "Okay, Aspen. Bedtime," she says. "Who do you want to read a story to you tonight?"

Aspen considers his options carefully. "Justin," he says.

Score one for the manny.

In his construction equipment pajamas, his teeth brushed, Aspen bounces up and down on his knees in bed. He doesn't look sleepy to me. "Two books," I say. "You want to pick them out?"

He comes back with a book about a kid picking blueberries right behind a bear. What are the people who write children's books thinking? Every page I turn I'm expecting something like, "Sal barely escaped with her life from the vicious mauling. And she never picked blueberries again." But no. Everybody eats blueberries and nobody gets killed or even maimed. Aspen's actually sitting still for this. I look over, and his eyes are half closed.

The second book's about a stray dog who finds a home. Aspen's just about out by the time I finish. I carefully maneuver his feet under the covers.

"I wanna go to the beach again tomorrow," Aspen mumbles.

"You got it."

"And you have to jump in."

"No way."

"Way."

He's pretty much asleep. I turn on the night-light.

"Good night," I say. "Don't let the lobsters bite."

I tiptoe out.

First thing I do is check my e-mail. Alex has written back.

To: justinb597@webmail.com
From: alxskywlkr@webmail.com
Subject: Re: Manny Mission Report #1

Report on mission objective received. Satisfactory progress.

This place = incredible. This team down the hall is making diamond semiconductors. In ten years all our computers will run on diamond chips. You don't believe me, but it's true.

Whatever gave you the idea that I don't believe you, Alex? I'm just not *interested*. As long as my computer comes on when I flip the switch, I couldn't care less whether it runs on silicon, diamonds, or unleaded.

Got assigned to my project today. It's X-ray diffusion. If you paid attention in science instead of cheating off me, you'd know that's an X-ray that goes through clothes but not skin. You got it—it lets you see people naked.

Maybe I *should* pay a little more attention in physics. On the other hand, I'm pretty sure Mr. Levy never mentioned anything like this.

It's for screening people at airports, so get your mind out of the gutter, Blakewell. They've got me working on some algorithm to block out the stuff you don't want your average

security worker to see. Especially for women. Know what I
mean?

Wait a minute. Who says a terrorist couldn't be hiding a
deadly weapon in her bra?

Wait a minute. You mean Alex is going to be spending his
entire summer looking at boobs?

I read the e-mail again. Yes, it's true. In the interests of national security, my friend gets to look at pictures of naked
women all day.

Life is truly unfair.

They threw a lunch for all the interns today. I sat next to this
redhead from NJ. Her name's Claire. There are a couple of
other girls around too. If the nanny thing doesn't work out
you can always go into computers.

Oh great. Geek chicks. Female versions of Alex. No
thanks.

Claire says she likes men who know how to program.
Alex

Hold on here. Alex is *not* supposed to be getting ahead of
me on the girl front. I haven't even talked to Serafina on the
phone, and he's already chatting with this girl about what
she likes in a man?

I can't e-mail him back before I've made some progress.
I've got to see Serafina again and get her number. I'm only
in the Hamptons for a month, after all. I don't have time to
waste.

Chapter 8

DON'T GET ME WRONG. Most of the time Aspen's a pretty cool little kid. I like him.

Just not right now.

"I wanna go *out*," he says for the twentieth time in the last ten minutes. Somehow he manages to give the word *out* at least five syllables.

"We can't go out," I say, for the twenty-first time. "It's raining."

It's Monday afternoon, and it's been raining all day, this nasty, steady drizzle. It doesn't seem too bad when you look out the window, but the wind's blowing in six different directions at once and the minute you go outside, rain gets blown down your neck, inside your jacket, in your face. Any sensible person would see that it's a good day to stay indoors.

Aspen, of course, is not sensible. He's four. He sits there pouting, and all of a sudden he throws out a hand and knocks down the tower of blocks we've been building.

"Hey!" I protest. "What'd you do that for?"

Because he can't go outside, of course. Stupid question. But he's too young to figure that out, so he just sits there and scowls.

"Knocking the blocks over isn't going to make it stop raining," I point out. "Okay. You're done with blocks. Want to do a puzzle?"

"No!"

"Want to draw a picture?"

"No!"

"Well, we'd better clean these blocks up anyway." I scoop a handful into the box and push another little pile over toward Aspen. "You get started on those."

Next thing I know a block goes flying across the room and hits the wall, smack.

"Aspen!" Mrs. B yells. She's busy in the kitchen, making something complicated for dinner. "Time out. In your bedroom, for ten minutes. *Now*."

Don't argue with an angry lady holding an eight-inch knife.

Aspen goes. Shuffling his feet. His lower lip's out so far you could balance a golf ball on it.

I wonder if Mrs. B is going to tell me I should have kept better control of Aspen. But she just goes back to chopping.

I put the blocks away. Since there's nothing else to do, I pick up a deck of cards and lay out a game of solitaire on the coffee table next to Mrs. B's new painting, which she still hasn't figured out where to hang.

I'm thirsty. I could get a glass of water, I guess. But what I really want is a Coke. Thinking about that bright red can, ice cold from the fridge, with little drops of water beading up on the outside, is making my mouth water.

This is stupid. Ms. Lasky never minds if I drink a soda out of her fridge when I'm babysitting Ian and Michael. Of course, Ms. Lasksy's not usually *around* when I'm babysitting Ian and Michael. Not like Mrs. B, who's right there in the kitchen, chopping away.

Still. I'm imagining the little *schock* noise the tab makes when you push it in, the hiss of air escaping, that first taste, the best one, when you hardly have to tilt the can. . . .

Somehow, I find myself standing in front of the refrigerator. Mrs. B looks over at me. She's stirring something in a pot.

"Ummm . . ." I thought I got over calling her that. "Can I have a Coke?"

The minute I ask, I know it sounds stupid. Like I'm no older than Aspen.

Mrs. B gives me a funny look. "Justin, you don't have to ask about every little thing." But she says it sort of impatiently, like I should have figured this out already. She waves a long wooden spoon around the kitchen. "Eat whatever you want. There's plenty."

I get my Coke and beat it back into the living room. I don't know why I'm all embarrassed. I just asked, right?

I go back to my solitaire game, careful to put my soda on a coaster so it won't leave a ring on the table, and to keep it far away from Mrs. B's painting. She put it facedown on some magazines so nothing would scratch the glass, which means that, as I flip over my first three cards, I can see the sticker on the back. Funny, it's not called *Exploding Eggplant* like you'd think. The sticker says *Sonata in Purple, #4.*

And that number below would be . . . the price.

I don't even notice that I've turned up an ace.

This thing costs more than three months' rent on the

apartment where my mom and I live. And it's less than two feet square. And it's *ugly*. And you can't do anything with it but hang it on a wall, if you can figure out which wall you want to hang it on.

I'm still staring at those four neat little numbers when the kitchen door slams. Mr. B must be back from the store.

"I said dill." I hear Mrs. B's voice from the kitchen.

"You said parsley."

"Why would I need parsley for a fish sauce?"

"I don't know, but that's what you said."

Mr. B's still in his coat, dripping water on the floor. Mrs. B's holding a big bunch of something green.

"Well, you'll have to go back."

"Gayle, it's beyond cats and dogs out there. It's raining dinosaurs. I'm not going back to the store because you told me the wrong herb."

Mrs. B throws the green stuff down on a cutting board and begins chopping it. Quick angry movements with the knife. I hope she's watching out for her fingers.

Mr. B takes off his coat and shakes water all over the floor.

"Kevin, be careful!"

"I'll clean it up."

He mops. My game of solitaire goes bust, and I lay out another one, trying to look like all I care about is whether I'll turn over a black eight to go on the red nine. But I'm expecting electric sparks to fly from all the tension. It's like when you shuffle your feet across the carpet in the winter and you know that the next thing you touch will give you a shock. And you can't spend the rest of your life without touching anything.

"The office called."

That's Mr. B. touching something.

"That Michelson deal is coming up. Maybe I'll take the train in tomorrow and see about it."

Chop, chop, chop.

"I thought you were taking this month off."

"I am. But if it's going to rain like this, I might as well go back in."

"So all you came out here for is the weather?"

The green stuff goes into a pot. She begins to work on an onion.

"Gayle, come on. Don't be like that."

"Like what? Like expecting my husband to spend some time with his family occasionally? Is that what I shouldn't be like?"

"Oh, and you didn't spend five weeks at the office on the Peters case? You came home to sleep occasionally."

I pick up my Coke and do my best to ooze out of the room without a sound. Although I doubt they'd have noticed if I wore army boots and stamped. I'm pretty sure Aspen's ten minutes are up. Maybe we can find something to do in his room until his parents either deal with their issues or go into counseling.

I can still hear them from the hallway. "That wasn't vacation. We were supposed to spend this time together. But if that's not important to you . . ."

Aspen's sitting on the floor by his bed. Not playing. Not reading. Not doing anything but sitting there.

"Hey, buddy. Want to build with blocks some more?"

He doesn't answer. I go and sit on the floor next to him.

"Grown-ups fight sometimes," I say, like I'm old and wise. "Don't worry about it. They'll stop in a little while."

I don't think he believes me.

"Hey, here's that bear book. You want to read that again?"

He doesn't say no. I take a swig of Coke to loosen up my voice, and suddenly a great big belch comes rolling up out of my gut. A little smile flickers across Aspen's face.

"Oh, you think that was funny? Here, listen to this." This is a skill I picked up in fifth grade. Of course, it's not something I do much these days. Doesn't really fit my image. But anything for a good cause.

I swallow a little bit of air, hold it for a minute to let it grow, and let out a good one. I swear it echoes.

Aspen laughs.

"Here, you try. Take a sip of Coke. It'll help get you started."

It takes him a few attempts, but he's a natural. Pretty soon he's belching like a pro.

"Excellent!" I applaud. And listen for a minute. I can't hear any more of the argument. Maybe they've made up. "Let's play War some more, how's that?"

When we're back out in the living room, I can see that I was overly optimistic about the fight being over. Mr. and Mrs. B aren't talking anymore, but they're still fighting. She's chopping vegetables like she's got a grudge against them. He's going over some papers on the table. The air practically sizzles.

Nobody says anything as Aspen and I sit down on the floor and I shuffle the cards. So when Aspen lets out a really good belch, it sure gets everybody's attention.

I forgot to tell him that belching is a talent best exercised elsewhere than in front of one's parents.

Mrs. B freezes with the knife two inches above the cutting board. Mr. B's head swivels around.

"Aspen!" Mrs. B gasps. "What do you say?"

"Justin taught me!" says Aspen.

Oh, great.

Mrs. B looks like she might use the knife on me.

"You think that's good?" Mr. B says all of a sudden. "Listen to this!"

He practically shakes the rafters. Aspen's mouth is open. I check. Mine is too. I shut it.

"Oh, yeah?" Mrs. B says, and drops the knife. "That's nothing."

And, I swear, *she* lets one out that puts his to shame.

And suddenly they're both laughing. Aspen and I look at each other, like the craziness of adults is beyond us. But I have to admit it's pretty funny. Now all four of us are laughing.

"Oh my goodness," Mrs. B says weakly. She's leaning over the counter. "Justin, what have you done?"

Hey, I didn't make her husband start sounding off like a brass band.

I start to say, "I didn't mean . . ." when, instead of the words, a belch pops out. Seriously, I didn't do it on purpose. It was all that Coke catching up with me. But it's the gold medal champion of all belches. Not just loud, but long, rumbling on and on like a freight train in a tunnel.

For a minute everybody just stares. Then we're all laughing like lunatics. Every now and then somebody pops out a little belch that starts us off all over again.

Chapter 9

By the next day, the rain's stopped. In the morning, Mrs. B takes Aspen with her on some errands, and after lunch the two of us hit the beach. There aren't that many other kids playing around the old dock. No sign of Serafina or even her friend Liz.

A guy in cutoff jeans and a beat-up sweatshirt is throwing a Frisbee for his black lab. For Aspen, this is as good a spectator sport as the Super Bowl. He jumps up and down and shrieks in that eardrum-damaging pitch every time the dog makes a catch.

This can hardly fail to attract the attention of sweatshirt guy, and he grins and holds the Frisbee out to Aspen. "You want to throw it for her?" He glances over at me. "She's real friendly," he adds. "She loves kids."

Aspen can't throw the Frisbee more than a few feet, but the dog doesn't care. She pounces on the toy like she's bringing down a caribou to feed the pack for the winter and trots back to Aspen. It's hard to say which of them is happier.

"Drop, Lucky," sweatshirt guy says, but Lucky just stands there, gripping the Frisbee with her teeth and whapping her tail back and forth. "Dumb dog, nobody can throw it again until you let go," her owner complains. "Drop it, I said!"

She does, and Aspen gets to throw it about five more times before Lucky and sweatshirt guy jog on down the beach. Left to ourselves, Aspen and I venture into the water—about knee-deep for me and waist-deep for him. I grab his hands and swing him into the oncoming waves. He can't decide whether to scream or laugh, so he does both.

Then we build a sandcastle that's taller than he is. It's an architectural triumph, the Empire State Building of sand castles. I threaten to throw Aspen into the water to wash off all the sand, which of course leads to more of the running and chasing thing that we did last time. It's okay for the first ten minutes or so, but frankly, after that, Aspen gets more out of it than I do.

I flop down on my towel, gasping for breath.

"Chase me more!" Aspen orders.

"No way," I wheeze.

"Way! Way!"

Did somebody plug this kid into a battery or something? Where does he get all this energy? I look at him and no-tice he's starting to turn a little pink across the tops of his shoulders.

"Okay, it's going to be time to head home soon, buddy." I dig his red T-shirt out of my backpack and throw it in his di-rection. He doesn't even try to catch it. "Put your shirt on," I tell him.

"It's hot," he whines. "I don't want my shirt on."

What happened to the running, laughing little maniac I had on my hands a few minutes ago? Suddenly Aspen's got that golf-ball pout back on his face, scowling down at the shirt lying in the sand at his feet.

"Look, you're starting to get sunburned," I explain patiently. I already know, however, that logic is wasted on a four-year-old, so I move directly on to threats. "If you put your shirt on, you can play a few more minutes. If you don't, we're leaving right now."

Aspen pulls the shirt on with an elaborate display of reluctance. It's kind of like somebody took a movie of a little kid getting dressed and then ran it in slow motion. He's got one arm in the sleeve and the neck hole halfway down over his face when something big and black pounces at his feet, scattering sand everywhere. It's that dog, Lucky.

Lucky jumps around at Aspen's feet, her big paws splayed out, her tail lashing back and forth, saying, "Play with me, play with me, I just can't stand it if you don't play with me" in dog language. But her cherished Frisbee is gone. Aspen, stuck halfway into his shirt, begins to laugh. Then he starts to pull the shirt back off.

"Put your shirt on, Aspen," I say, spitting sand out from between my teeth and getting up to look around for sweatshirt guy. He's nowhere to be seen.

When I look back, Aspen still doesn't have his shirt on. In fact, progress has been retrograde. Now he's holding the shirt out at arm's length, right above Lucky's nose. Lucky's clearly beside herself with joy at the thought of something new to chew on.

"Aspen!" I say loudly. "I said put your shirt on!"

Aspen looks at me, I swear, with a calculating eye, like he's a bank robber and I'm a cop, and he's trying to decide if I'm really going to shoot.

"Aspen!" I say even louder. "If you give your shirt to that dog, we are *leaving* this beach!"

Aspen drops the shirt. Lucky pounces. She snatches it up in her teeth and shakes it from side to side ferociously. Apparently she thinks it's a dangerous snake and it's her duty to snap its spine before it can bite anybody.

I lunge forward and grab her collar. I get my other hand on Aspen's shirt, but Lucky braces her feet for a tug of war, and I'm afraid that the stitches will give. How did sweatshirt guy get her to give something up?

"Drop it!" I say sternly, trying to sound just like her owner. "Lucky, drop!"

She does. I snatch the shirt up, and she looks at me expectantly. What does she want? Oh yeah. "Good dog," I say.

Aspen's giggling. "She ate my shirt! She ate my shirt!" he says, ecstatic.

"Yeah? No kidding!" I see sweatshirt dude now, way down the beach, and give Lucky a shove in his direction. "Go on, shoo!" I tell her. "Run! Move!" She looks confused at first and then gets the idea and takes off, spraying sand all over Aspen and me.

"Okay." I throw the dog-chewed shirt back at Aspen. "I told you to put your shirt on. I told you not to let the dog have your shirt. So put it on now, because we're leaving."

Aspen's face crumples.

"I don't want to leave!" he howls, full volume. "I don't want my shirt!"

I don't answer. I just stare at him. This is a technique I learned from Ian and Michael. Most people can't stand to be just looked at, and little kids are no exception. Sure enough,

Aspen simmers down and looks nervously at me, to see why I've lost the power of speech.

I pick up his shirt, turn it right side out, and pull it down over his head. I let him find the armholes for himself while I stuff towels, drinks, and the rest of his beach paraphernalia into my backpack.

For a minute it looks like things will remain calm. But then Aspen makes a discovery about the shirt.

"It's wet!" He looks up at me, panicked. "My shirt's wet! It's *dog drool*!"

"Well, yeah," I agree, zipping up the backpack. "That's because you let a dog chew on it."

"I can't wear it! It's got *dog drool* on it!"

"So next time you won't give it to a dog when I tell you not to." I pick up the backpack and hold out my hand. "Let's go."

Of course, it's not that simple. He gets hold of the wet patch on his shirt with one hand, pulls it away from his chest so that the dog drool won't touch his bare skin, and starts to cry.

I have no sympathy. I get hold of his free hand and start towing him up the beach, back toward the parking lot. We're just about to the bike when I spot the last person I want to see right now. Serafina, with Molly in a stroller.

Just perfect.

"Justin? Is everything all right?" she asks, looking at us curiously.

"Yeah, nothing serious," I tell her.

"My shirt's got *dog drool*," Aspen whimpers.

"Oh no," she says soberly. "That's terrible. Show me where."

Aspen's crying scales itself down to sniffling as Serafina

crouches down in front of him. Heck, if she was that close to me, I wouldn't be crying either. He shows her the wet patch, which he still has gripped in his fist. She looks at it like she's a doctor considering symptoms of bubonic plague. Then she takes a bottle of water out of the stroller and dribbles a little on the front of Aspen's shirt until you can't tell where the original wet spot of dog drool started.

"All clean now. How's that?" she says, and smiles.

Aspen sniffs hard and tucks his chin down to look at his shirt.

"And here." Serafina pulls a box of animal crackers out from underneath Molly's stroller. She shows two of them to Aspen. "An elephant and a monkey. Which do you want?"

Aspen, still pouting but no longer crying, picks the elephant. Serafina gives him the monkey too.

"Better now?" she asks.

He nods.

"It was all his own fault," I say. "He gave that shirt to a dog after I specifically told him not to. I wasn't being mean to him. I love kids, I can't wait to have a bushel of my own someday." No, all right, I don't actually say any of that.

"Uh, thanks," is what I really say. "Aspen, say thank you."

"Thank you," Aspen mumbles through a mouthful of animal cracker.

"Are you leaving the beach already?" Serafina says.

"Yeah," I say, without getting into why. I mean, I'd love to hang out at the beach with Serafina again, no question. I can catch a glimpse of that pink bathing suit under her white T-shirt. But I told Aspen we were leaving if he gave his shirt to the dog, so we're leaving.

But before we go . . .

"Uh," I say to Serafina. "Maybe . . ." I'm not going to blow this again. I'm not. I take a deep breath and get out the hardest six words in the English language. "Maybe I can call you sometime?"

The minute I say it, I realize it's all wrong. I'm sweaty and sandy and sticky, towing a whimpering child by the hand. I'm about as far from suave as one person can get. Stupid, stupid, *stupid*. Why didn't I wait for a better time? Now I've spoiled everything. Serafina will never—

What's that she's holding out to me?

I take the little scrap of paper from her fingers. She's smiling.

"See you later," she says, and heads toward the beach with Molly.

That evening, after dinner's over and while Mr. B is giving Aspen his bath, I go into my room and shut the door. I don't give myself any time to get nervous before I dial the phone.

And hang up. Maybe I should wait until tomorrow. After all, when Serafina saw me today I wasn't exactly at my best. I should wait to call her until I've had the chance to create a better impression. Don't want to rush things and look desperate.

But it's already Tuesday night, the end of my fourth day in the Hamptons. I haven't got time to wait around. And there's also Alex's e-mail about the startling new direction his love life had taken. I've got to answer that, and I can't do it until I've called Serafina.

Enough stalling. I dial again, and this time I let the phone ring until somebody picks up.

"Hello?"

I'd know that voice anywhere. Soft, gentle, warm.

"Hi, Serafina. It's Justin. I was wondering—"

"No, this isn't Serafina. Hold on." I hear the person on the other end put down the phone and yell, "Fina! It's a *boy!*" I bet this never happens to Dillon.

There's a pause, and someone else picks up the phone.

"Hello?"

"Hi, it's Justin."

"Oh, hi."

Pause.

"So," I say. "Did you have fun at the beach today?" Oh, please. I sound like a Sunday school teacher.

"Yes."

"So," I say, before I remember that I said it before. "I mean . . ." Oh, stop it, I tell myself. Be a man. What did you call her for? "Do you want to go out tomorrow? Have dinner?"

There.

"Yes."

Apparently she only speaks in monosyllables on the phone. Wait a minute. What did she say?

"Yes? You mean you want to?"

"Yes, I do."

"Well. Good. I mean, how about . . ." I don't know this town. Where should I suggest? "How about Antonio's?" That place I saw on the way to the beach. It looked ritzy enough for Serafina.

"I don't know. I don't like Antonio's so much."

"You don't?" Is there a more expensive restaurant in town?

"What if we go to the beach? And have hot dogs at Jack's?"

"Well, sure. If you want." I'm having trouble giving up my vision of fine dining. A piano playing in the background. The valet parking the car that I don't have. The waiter carding me when I order a bottle of wine. Maybe Jack's isn't such a bad idea after all.

"Seven o'clock?" I suggest, trying to get back some control over this phone call.

"All right."

"See you then."

"All right."

"Bye."

She hangs up.

I go into the den and log on to e-mail so I can update Alex and Dillon on my progress. But I see an e-mail from my mom, so I open that first.

To: justin597@webmail.com
From: Lblakewell@walkerandco.com
Subject: You'll Never Guess

Honey—

You won't believe what happened. You remember the new guy at work I told you about? The one who's been stopping by my desk to chat? Yesterday he asked me if I wanted to get a bite to eat after work. I thought he meant a sandwich or something, but he'd made a reservation at a fancy place— champagne and everything. It's a little early to tell for sure, but he seems like a real Bugs. We're going out again on Thursday, so I'll let you know more!

love,

Mom

Bugs you can probably figure out for yourself. Bugs Bunny, smooth and suave, the coolest thing in the cartoon kingdom.

I hit REPLY and then sit there, tapping the keyboard until I realize I'm typing a line of z's all the way across the screen. What kind of a move is that, champagne on the first date? Some guy I've never met sweeping my mom off her feet, and she writes me e-mail like I'm supposed to be happy about it?

I close the e-mail without replying. I was going to give Alex and Dillon a detailed report of the manny mission and my upcoming date with Serafina, but now I don't feel like it. I address an e-mail to both of them, but all I type is one sentence.

To: alxskywlkr@webmail.com
To: playboy311@netwave.com
From: justin597@webmail.com
Subject: Manny Mission Report #2

Target in sight.

Chapter 10

WEDNESDAY NIGHT, Aspen insists on hanging around in my room while I pick out my clothes for the date. My best chinos, washed just the right number of times so they're a little soft, not too pressed. My blue shirt. Black high tops. A little gel for the piece of my hair that sticks up.

Aspen watches all this like there might be a pop quiz later. "Can I have some?" he asks. "In my hair like that?"

I work about half a teaspoon of gel into his hair and make him a little Mohawk, then hold him up to the mirror so he can see. He grins.

"Go show your mom and dad," I tell him.

He runs out of the room yelling.

I've still got fifteen minutes left before I can leave. I want to be a little early; I can't get away with making girls wait like Dillon does. But not so early that I look pathetic. When to show up for a date is a carefully calibrated science.

I check e-mail to kill the time. Nothing from my mom or Alex. One from Dillon.

To: justin597@webmail.com
From: playboy311@netwave.com
Subject: 'sup?

---

kendra found out abt ana so thats dead 4 the summer

emily from algebra still hot tho

u?

Dillon doesn't believe in wasting effort. He won't move a finger to tap a key unless he absolutely has to.

I close the window. I'll answer him later, after I've got something real to report.

I get the timing perfect. I make it to the beach, lock up the bike, stroll down to Jack's, and get there just a couple of minutes before Serafina arrives.

Serafina looks . . .

I don't have to tell you what Serafina looks like, do I? I mean, you get the idea by now.

The sunlight touches Serafina's skin gently. She has on a white sleeveless shirt. There's a little lace around the scooped neck that brushes against smooth skin the color of cinnamon. A cool breeze coming off the ocean will be the perfect excuse for offering her my jacket later on.

"Hello," she says. Still the best word in the language.

"Hi."

Pause.

"So, are you hungry?"

She nods.

We get in line. Serafina orders a chicken salad. I get a hot dog.

"Here you go," says the guy, handing us our food through the little window. "Best on the beach, served by Jack himself. Tell all your friends."

Serafina and I find a spot at one of the picnic tables. We sit there, looking out at the water and eating.

So far, all I've established is that she wanted Diet Coke with her salad and that she doesn't eat fries. I want to say, "Tell me everything about you. Tell me all your deepest secrets. Tell me what you want out of life. Tell me what hurts you, what makes you happy."

I eat another french fry.

"I love the ocean," Serafina says, looking out at the white-caps and the gulls swooping and squawking.

"Yeah, me too." I don't really. I mean, I don't hate the ocean or anything. I don't have cruel feelings toward it. But love it? It's cold and fishy and, well, wet. It's a lot of water in one place. I can't figure out why people get all emotional about it.

"Isn't the light beautiful?"

"Yeah," I say, looking at the way the light falls on her cheekbones.

"In Argentina, the light is like this in the mountains," she says, remembering. "Where my grandparents live. We go there every winter; of course, it's summer there when it's winter here. And you can see how it's dark in the valleys, but it stays light forever up in the mountains."

"Do you miss it?"

She shrugs. It's still charming.

"I was only five when we left. My father says I can't really remember anything."

"But can you?"

I'm looking at her. She's looking out at the water, at the seagulls dive-bombing the waves.

"I remember our house, I think. There was a yellow cat who lived in the front yard. Our cook fed him in the kitchen, and I used to pet him. And I remember the plane ride when we left. I'm sure about that. My mother cried."

A breeze comes up and blows her hair. She shivers a little. Just like I planned, I take my jacket off and slip it over her shoulders. She smiles.

This is what it's about. Guys at school chase girls around and brag about hooking up, counting up their scores, like it's some great accomplishment to get a girl so drunk she doesn't realize what an ass you are. Even Dillon sometimes acts like there's no difference between a girl and a pair of socks—lose one, just get another.

But this is the important part: the way, when you're with a girl as beautiful as Serafina, everything in you feels alive. Like you're a radio, tuned to her frequency. Every little move she makes—tucking a strand of hair behind her ear, hugging my jacket closer around her—touches me, sets something inside me humming like a tuning fork.

She reaches over and takes one of my fries.

"Hey," I say, trying to keep it light. I don't want her to see how that little move sent me spinning. "I thought you didn't like fries."

"I do like them." She bites off the end. "I don't buy them.

They are too fattening. But they taste good. So I eat the ones my friends buy."

Girl logic.

"Now it's your turn." She looks at me. "To talk about yourself."

What am I going to tell her? I think about my apartment. I try to imagine her visiting me there, watching TV on the couch with the broken springs.

"You have to tell me something. Do you have any brothers and sisters?"

Good, an easy one. "No, it's just me and my mom."

"Your parents are divorced?"

"No, my dad died."

"I am very sorry." And she really looks sorry, and worried that she shouldn't have brought it up. "That's sad."

"It's sad for my mom." I shrug. "I didn't really know him, so I can't miss him."

"But don't you wonder? How much of him is in you? It must be strange, knowing that you are like someone you don't remember."

How did she know? How did she know that I wonder about that? When I look in the mirror to part my hair, I wonder if he had that cowlick like mine. He was six feet one; I'm five nine. I wonder if I'll get as tall as he was. I wonder if he wanted something more for his life than a one-bedroom apartment in Queens.

"Like your hair." She reaches out to touch the little piece of hair over my forehead. "Did his hair do that too?"

I'm too startled at the way she read my mind to answer for a minute. Before I can get my mouth in gear, she waves to somebody. A bunch of somebodies, actually. A group of five kids. Tall guy, thinking he looks cool in a leather jacket. Shorter guy. Three girls.

Serafina's smiling. Like she doesn't even notice that all these people have intruded on our tender moment.

"Carter, Josh. Caitlyn, Kath, Autumn. This is Justin."

I nod. They nod back. When are they going to move on?

"Did you hear about Jenna's parents?" one of the girls— Autumn, I think—says. Who gets named after a season?

"No, what?"

"It's true about the massage therapist. Can you believe?"

Pretty soon they're deep in conversation about the personal problems of the parents of somebody I never even met.

"Are you new here this summer?" Kath, who's got curly red-gold hair and freckles, tries to make an effort. "I haven't seen you around."

"Yeah, I only got here on Saturday. And I work during the days."

"What kind of work?"

"I'm a—" Well, it's not like Serafina doesn't already know. And who cares about the rest of them? "I'm taking care of a kid."

Carter hears me.

"You're a nanny?" I think about telling him the term is "manny," and about how it's a trend and about *Friends* and everything, but frankly, I don't feel like having that much of a conversation with him. Carter stops his smile before it spreads too far. "That's—great. Yeah. Fina, we're going up to the Silver Bullet, you want to come? I've got my car."

He doesn't ask me if I want to come, I notice. He gestures

toward the parking lot. A dark red convertible. That's his car?

Maybe Serafina gets that I'm a little irritated, because she shakes her head quickly.

"No, thank you," she says.

"We have plans," I add, waiting for Carter and his crowd to get the hint.

He doesn't.

"Okay. But you're coming on Friday, right? To the party?" Carter turns to look at me. "You want to come too? My parents are out of town."

A parent-free party in the Hamptons? I quickly revise my opinion of Carter. He's all right. Even though he turns back to Serafina without waiting for my answer.

"Of course," Serafina says.

"Yeah, thanks," I put in.

"Okay. Later." Obviously Carter's the leader of this pack. When he moves off, they all follow. The girls wave. Serafina and I sit.

"What plans?" she asks.

"What?"

"You said we had plans. What plans do we have?"

Ummm . . .

"A walk on the beach?" I say desperately.

"How nice."

She really seems to mean it.

She keeps my jacket on for all of our slow wander down the beach and back. We don't talk that much, but it feels fine just to be next to her.

I walk her back to her car. She slips my jacket off and

hands it to me. I fold it over on my arm. I can feel the warmth of her skin in the lining.

Would she mind? Maybe the first date is too early. Maybe I should wait for the second. Wait, our second date's going to be that party at what's his name's, Carter's. It'll probably be crowded. Lots of people around, watching. Not a great spot for the first kiss.

She tips her head to one side just a little, looking at me. Is that a hint? Why don't girls come with instructions?

"I'll call you tomorrow," she says. "About the party."

"Okay." I start to lean in a little closer, but she's already turning to get in the car, so all I get is the brush of her hair across my face and the smell of strawberry shampoo. I dodge back so I don't get hit by the car door when she opens it and so she (hopefully) doesn't notice my less-than-slick first-kiss technique.

She drives off, waving out the window as she pauses for a stop sign.

I get my bike, I mean Mr. B's bike, and ride back to the Beltons' cottage, thinking about Serafina's car. It's not a flashy convertible like Carter's. It's just a nice little Honda. Much nicer than the car I don't have. I stand up to push the bike hard, feeling the strain in my calves, in my lungs.

Am I supposed to pick Serafina up for the party tomorrow? How am I going to do that with no vehicle that has more than two wheels? It was okay for Jack's, but Carter is obviously part of the rich crowd. I imagine the driveway in front of his house crammed with convertibles, Jeeps, Hummers. By the time I'm at the Beltons', I have to stop and lean over the handlebars for a minute to catch my breath.

Before I go to bed I go into the den, turn on the computer, and hit REPLY to Dillon's e-mail. I address it to Alex too.

To: playboy311@netwave.com
To: alxskywlker@webmail.com
From: justin597@webmail.com
Re: re: 'sup?

Serafina's the hottest thing on the beach. She was wearing this white sleeveless shirt and it made her skin look

I can't quite figure out how to finish that sentence. I'll come back to it.

We talked about her home in Argentina and about my dad. But then

I don't feel like getting into that whole thing about Carter and his friends. Lackeys. Hangers-on. I know the type.

Taking her to a party on Friday. Will let you know progress.

I hit SEND before I remember to go back and finish a couple of the sentences.

Chapter 11

IT'S REAL LIFE AGAIN ON THURSDAY. No more girls with cinnamon-colored skin and dark velvet hair. Just me hanging out on the back deck after breakfast, killing time before I have to take Aspen to his swim lesson.

Yesterday Mr. and Mrs. B went to a plant nursery and brought home a bunch of bushes with big pink flowers. Now Mr. B is digging holes for the bushes to go in. Aspen has a trowel, and he's helping. Well, sort of. He's probably knocking more dirt back into the hole than he's taking out, but Mr. B doesn't seem to care. As for me, I'm sitting on the steps, enjoying the always-pleasant sight of somebody working harder than I am.

Funny, I never realized before how Mr. B's hair is the same color as Aspen's. You don't notice at first because Aspen's hair is cut in this retro 1960s bowl style, and Mr. B's is neat and trim, an inch long at most. But it's exactly the same shade of brown with just a bit of red in it.

That little piece of my hair in front is sticking up again as it dries after my shower. I lick my fingers and try to press it back down.

But don't you wonder? How much of him is in you?

Yeah, I wonder. I wonder all the time, actually. It's just that I don't talk about it much. I can't bring this stuff up with my mom; I don't want to upset her. And Dillon and I mostly talk about girls, and about cool places to take the girls, and about clothes to wear when you take the girls to the cool places.

Sometimes I tell Alex a few of the things I think about my dad. But even though Alex doesn't get along with his father, at least the guy's *around*. At least Alex knows what he's like.

Alex doesn't get what it's like just not to know. He doesn't get how you can miss somebody who's never even been there.

"Come on, Justin," Mr. B says. "We could really use a hand."

Hey, they hired me to look after their kid. My contract doesn't include hard manual labor in the backyard.

But I get the other shovel and help out anyway. We get all three bushes planted before it's time for me to take Aspen to the pool.

As manny tasks go, swim lesson duty is not bad. I settle down on a chair by the side of the pool, put on my sharp-looking sunglasses, and watch Aspen and about ten other little kids hang on to the side of the pool and kick their feet for all they're worth.

Well, I'm not watching the little kids all the time. The swimming teacher is female, maybe twenty, and not bad to look at. And there are girls all around. None of them are Serafina. But there's still plenty to feast my eyes on. Another good thing about sunglasses—not only do they make you look cool, but they also let you stare at whoever you want, and nobody can tell.

A little crowd of girls strolls past. One of them looks like what's-her-name, Kath, from the beach last night. The one who actually tried talking to me. I can hear a little bit of what they're saying.

"Actually *saw* him . . ."

"Who?"

"You know, that guy from that movie . . ."

"Seriously hot . . ."

". . . down on Main Street . . ."

They spread their towels out not too far away from me, laughing, putting on suntan lotion. Kath pulls a big straw hat out of a bag.

"It's not fair, you guys tan so nice, all I do is freckle and peel."

She puts the hat on and slips the strap of her bathing suit down over one shoulder so one of her friends can rub lotion on her back.

Do girls *know* what that does to a guy?

"Justin! Justin!" Aspen's jumping up and down in front of me, trying to get my attention. I blink and come back down to earth.

"Uh . . . hey, buddy. Swim lesson over?"

"Watch me dive," Aspen commands. "Come and watch me dive, Justin. I can dive now. Come and watch me."

"Yeah, okay." I get up, push my sunglasses on top of my head, and follow Aspen over to the shallow end. He sits on the edge. I get in, waist-deep, so I can monitor his athletic achievement more closely.

Aspen scowls with concentration. He clasps his hands together over his head and slowly bends over at the waist until he does a bellyflop into the water. I grab for his hands as he comes up spluttering.

"Did you see?" he gargles. "Did you see me dive?"

"Sure, I did." I was standing a foot away, after all. I hold his hands until he gets his toes on the bottom of the pool. "Want to do it again?"

Aspen probably has about six gallons of chlorinated water up his nose by the time he's tired of diving. I become a sea monster for a while and chase him around. Then he wants a ride on the sea monster's back. Now *I've* got half of the water in the pool up my nose.

"Are these your sunglasses?" I hear somebody saying when I come up for air.

I blink water out of my eyes. Kath is sitting on the edge, holding out a pair of sunglasses. I pat the top of my head. Stupid. I forgot I had my glasses on when I became the Kraken, terror of the deep.

"Yeah, I guess so." I take the glasses from her.

"Another ride!" Aspen's pulling at the leg of my swimming trunks.

"Just a minute, buddy. Thanks," I say to Kath. She smiles. She's not bad-looking, actually. For all her complaining, she's got that soft, light skin that sometimes goes with red hair. And not as many freckles as she seems to think.

"I saw you on the beach, right?" she says. "You're Fina's friend."

"Yeah, that's right." I detach Aspen's hand from my trunks before he reveals more of me than I care to have exposed before the female population of the Hamptons. I turn back to Kath, planning on asking some smooth and suave questions—So, you come here every year? Have you known Serafina long?

"See you around, maybe," she says. She smiles, slides into the water, and swims off toward the deep end.

Oh well. At least I get to watch her swim away. Not a bad view at all. Very neat. Minimal splashing.

"Okay, Aspen. You want another ride?"

I don't see him.

Just a second ago, I was holding his hand. Well, a few seconds, maybe. It couldn't have been half a minute. I look down at my palm as if I'm still expecting to see Aspen's hand there. I don't even remember letting go.

I look around. Blond kids, black-haired kids. Little girls with ponytails. Boys with purple trunks, green trunks, striped trunks. No brown-haired little kid in blue trunks who doesn't even know how to dive yet.

Okay. Shit. Okay. Don't panic. Get the lifeguard to call out his name. That's what you do. It'll only take a few minutes. He can't be far.

A few minutes. Can't you get brain damage in thirty seconds or less? Don't they always say a person can drown in two inches of water? It's twelve feet over there in the deep end.

Shut *up*. Just get out and get the lifeguard. Don't think about it. Just move. Don't think—

"Justin! Look!"

The voice comes from behind me.

I guess with all that panicking I forgot to turn around.

Aspen's just a few feet away. He's got both arms clasped around a bright green beach ball. He bobs up and down, hanging on to it, like a buoy out in the ocean.

"Aspen!" I snarl. I'm amazed to hear my own voice. I sound really mean. I sound like every teacher I ever pissed off. I sound like my mom the day she got home from work and found me feeding Legos to the garbage disposal.

By now I've grabbed hold of Aspen's arm just above the elbow. Maybe I'm squeezing a little too hard. His eyes go wide and then squinch up.

"Don't *ever*—" I start to say, and then I stop.

Don't ever do—what? What did the kid do, exactly, that I'm yelling at him? He didn't run away or hide from me on purpose. He didn't even wander off. He wasn't more than five feet away from me the entire time.

What he did was make me feel worse than Brittany Westover did the time she kissed me in a closet at her birthday party and then told the whole fifth grade I had anchovy breath. Which wasn't true. I don't even like anchovies.

But Aspen didn't do this to me on purpose. I was talking to Kath. I wasn't watching him. Is that his fault?

"Sorry. Sorry, buddy." I loosen up my hold on his arm. "I just . . . I couldn't see you for a minute."

He bobs there, hanging on to the beach ball, like he's not sure if he's in trouble or not.

"Where'd you get that ball?" I ask, trying to get us back to normal. I can feel the adrenaline draining out of my veins. I think if I got out of the pool and tried to walk somewhere, my knees would shake.

"It's ours," says a voice I recognize.

Liz is holding Max on her hip and smiling.

Aspen and I play catch for a while with Liz and Max. I make Aspen laugh by diving spectacularly for long shots, falling into the water and splashing everybody nearby. I think he's forgotten that I turned into the manny from hell for a minute.

Then we take Aspen and Max over to the kiddie pool, a shallow little circle with a fountain in the middle. They run back and forth through the spray, shrieking. Liz and I sit on the edge to watch.

"So how'd the big date go last night?" Liz asks.

I've learned my lesson. I don't take my eyes off Aspen, even though it means I have to talk to Liz without looking at her. Luckily it's not that much of a temptation to look at Liz. Her swimsuit used to be dark blue, but now it's faded. Her wet hair's drying in the sun and sticks out in every direction.

"How'd you know about the date?" I ask her.

"Fina told me, of course." Liz doesn't look at me either. It's like we're in the prison yard and we don't want anyone to know we're talking. Planning our big breakout for midnight tonight. Bribe the guards, tunnel under the wall. . . .

"Girls talk to each other, you know," Liz goes on. "We're not like guys. We don't communicate in a series of grunts. So. How'd it go?"

It's none of her business, really. But I'm thinking about what she said . . . *girls talk*. This is true. Half the time girls aren't even paying attention to what's going on in front of them because they're thinking about how they'll describe it later on to their friends. The first time I kissed a girl (I mean really kissed; Brittany Westover doesn't count), she excused herself a minute later and went out of the room. I thought she was going to the bathroom or something. Turned out she was on her cell phone, giving her best friend a play-by-play.

So—obviously—Serafina talks about me to Liz. This could be useful.

"Didn't Serafina tell you how it went?" I ask. Subtly, I hope.

"Haven't seen her today. Hey, Max, no running!" she yells.

"But didn't she . . . I mean, last night . . ." So much for subtlety.

Liz gives me a quick glance before she looks back at the kids again. "Why don't you just ask me?"

"Ask you?"

"If she likes you."

"Why don't you just tell me?" I'm getting a little irritated. What kind of game does she think she's playing? I know something you don't know? Anyway, we're not in kindergarten anymore. We don't have to communicate in coded signals, like shoving a girl off the monkey bars to show you're interested. Serafina went on a date with me. She's going to a party with me tomorrow. I think she probably likes me.

"Yeah, she likes you."

"Really?" I ask pathetically.

Liz starts laughing. "Yeah, really, genius. Look. It's not like she doesn't get asked out a lot. Guys . . . well. But she doesn't have a boyfriend right now. So you've got a chance."

"What did she say about me?" I ask eagerly. This is great.

"I can't tell you that." She looks over at my face and starts laughing again. "It's a girl solidarity thing. It's privileged information, like with a lawyer or something."

"But you're going to tell her everything I said to you," I argue.

"Of course."

"That's not fair."

"It's dating. Who said it was fair?" She seems to take a little pity on me. "Look. I won't tell her you got all junior high over whether she likes you or not. How's that?"

"Great, thanks." I hope she can tell that was sarcastic.

"And I'll help you out if I can."

Really? I look over at her. The sun has brought out a light red flush over the tops of her cheekbones. She's squinting a little because of the light reflecting off the water.

"Here," I say, and hand her my sunglasses. "You want these?"

"Thanks." She puts them on. There are some girls who look like royalty or something the minute they put on a pair of sunglasses. Mysterious, fascinating. Liz isn't one of them. She just looks like Liz wearing sunglasses.

Except I can't tell where she's looking now. Over at Max? Sideways at me?

"So what do you want to know?"

Before I can figure out what to ask her, someone screams.

We look over at the main pool to see a guy throwing a girl into the water. The girl's got red hair. The guy, of course, is . . .

"Carter," Liz says in disgust.

"You don't like him, huh?"

"Not really." I can hear in her voice that it's an understatement.

"Serafina does, though?"

Liz shrugs. "Serafina likes everybody. Anyway, she hangs around with the crowd. She sees them every summer."

"I guess she's rich like them."

I say it before I even think about it. Before I realize how disloyal it sounds. But Liz doesn't seem surprised.

"Yeah," she says quietly. She pulls her fingers through her hair, tugging out the snarls. "It makes a difference, doesn't it? I live out here, I see the summer people every year. But I've never spent so much time around them as this summer. It's weird."

"They don't even realize how weird."

"That's the funny part." Liz starts to smile. "They think this is normal, the way they live."

"Beach *cottages*."

"Convertibles."

"Fresh dill for the fish sauce."

We're both laughing. "Anyway, it doesn't matter," Liz says. "Fina doesn't go out with Carter anymore."

What? Does that mean she went out with him *at one time*? "Did she . . ."

"A couple of weeks last summer. But don't worry about it."

A rich guy with a convertible who went out with Serafina last summer and I'm not supposed to worry about it? Me, riding to our dates on Mr. Belton's bike? Oh, right.

Kath is yelling that Carter's an idiot. She's trying to climb out, and he tosses her in again. The lifeguard blows his whistle.

"How could she . . ."

"Carter can put on a good act." Liz shrugs. "I think that's enough sun for Max." She stands up and calls to him.

"Wait a minute . . ." I say. But she's already drying Max off and getting his shirt on.

"What a minute what?" Liz asks, concentrating on getting Max's head and arms into the right holes.

"There's a party at Carter's," I blurt out. "Tomorrow. Serafina's going. Maybe you could . . ." I honestly have no idea how to get to the end of that sentence.

"IM me," Liz says. "Not tonight, Max's parents are going out and I have to watch him. Try me tomorrow morning. I'm queenelizabeth, it's all one word."

Looks like the manny mission has acquired a spy.

Chapter 12

FRIDAY. The day of Carter's party. My second date with Serafina. And not incidentally, my day off.

The first thing I do is sleep past that 8:00 A.M. breakfast. It's about 10:00 when I finally stumble downstairs for some food. The second thing I do is sit down at the computer, all ready to make contact with my spy.

The first date with Serafina went pretty well, even if I didn't get to kiss her. But this second date's going to be different. At a party for one thing. It's not like I've been raised in a closet or anything. I've been to social functions before. But this isn't the kind of party I usually go to, any more than Serafina's the kind of girl I usually date. Any bit of information Liz can give me could be helpful.

There's an e-mail from Dillon and one from my mom, but I save those for later and open up an IM window.

justintime (10:39:35 AM): Hey, your majesty. You online?

She must have been sitting at the computer, because the response pops right back up.

queenelizabeth (*10:40:12* AM): i'm here what's up?

justintime (10:41:48 AM): So your real name's Elizabeth? Guess I could have figured that out. But Liz seems right for you. Can't imagine anybody calling you Elizabeth.

queenelizabeth (*10:42:52* AM): teachers call me Elizabeth b/c that's how I sign my papers but at home and in the summer I'm Liz.

justintime (10:43:14 AM): So tell me stuff about Serafina.

queenelizabeth (*10:43:57* AM): no fair just saying tell you stuff. what do u want to know?

justintime (10:45:26 AM): I dunno, everything! Like what she eats for breakfast and what's her favorite color and what does she want in a man and why did she break up with Carter?

queenelizabeth (*10:46:49* AM): 1) nothing. 2) red. 3) what we all want—romance & excitement & sensitivity & honesty & gentleness & intelligence & good looks & sense of humor. In other words, what doesn't exist. 4) b/c he's a jerk. (U could have figured that out 2.)

queenelizabeth (*10:47:03* AM): Probably shouldn't have told you about Carter and Fina don't mention it to her OK?

justintime (10:48:52 AM): Hey would go to jail to protect sources. Don't worry about it. You really think there are no guys like you described?

queenelizabeth (*10:49:39* AM): haven't met one yet

justintime (10:50:46 AM): So why are you helping me with Serafina if you don't think guys are any good?

queenelizabeth (*10:52:58* AM): don't get all offended. just meant that when it comes to romance we all want more than can be possible. girls and guys too. that's y everybody's always unhappy about it.

justintime (10:54:24 AM): Not always unhappy. Yeah you have to risk getting your heart broken. But it's worth it for all the good stuff.

queenelizabeth (10:55:29 AM): don't have to get ur heart broken if u don't expect more than can possibly be there. that's what i'm saying. anyway aren't you supposed to be asking me about Fina?

justintime (10:56:08 AM): Yeah you going to this party at Carter's?

queenelizabeth (10:56:51 AM): no way

justintime (10:57:08 AM): y not?

queenelizabeth (10:58:52 AM): not invited. not my kind of thing anyway. u should see his parents' place, tho. 3 houses down from where I work. all it needs is a moat and a draw-bridge.

justintime (11:00:36 AM): There going to be lots of people there?

queenelizabeth (11:01:17 AM): how should I know? i didn't see the guest list. probably. carter's family's been coming here in the summers since the mayflower. they know pretty much everybody, everybody with money, I mean.

justintime (11:03:25 AM): So tell me more about Serafina. How can I impress her?

queenelizabeth (11:05:49 AM): not rocket science. don't know why you guys have such a hard time w/ this. treat her nice. pay attention when she talks. don't get drunk at the party, she hates that. nothing more boring than hanging out with some guy who can't see straight.

justintime (11:06:10 AM): got it

queenelizabeth (11:06:52 AM): and she likes to dance

queenelizabeth (*11:08:13 AM*): justin? u there?

queenelizabeth (*11:09:06 AM*): u can't dance can u?

justintime (11:10:02 AM): sure I can dance no problem disco fever

queenelizabeth (*11:10:47 AM*): ok just telling you. listen i have to go play w/max. talk to u later ok?

justintime (11:11:13 AM): ok later

Well, I guess that was helpful. Some of it, anyway. I sort of wish Liz was going to the party too, though. It'd be good to have someone else there who's not part of Carter's crowd. Carter, whose family's been coming out here for the summers since the *Mayflower*.

I wonder why she's so down on dating, though. Like there's no such thing as romance in the world. Maybe she just hasn't met the right guy yet. If she felt about a guy the way I feel about Serafina, then she'd know that you *can't* expect too much. That nothing you can expect could equal the way you feel when everything goes right.

I open up Dillon's e-mail.

To: justinb597@webmail.com
From: playboy311@netwave.com
Subject: watch out

what u mean u talked abt ur dad? girls dont = big drama. just girls. u always get 2 serious, blakewell. scares them off.

Dillon always thinks he's the Ann Landers of dating. You don't even have to ask him for his advice; he offers it free.

Sometimes it gets on my nerves. Like right now. I hit REPLY and type as quickly as I can.

To: playboy311@netwave.com
From: justinb597@webmail.com
Subject: Re: watch out

Yeah you don't scare yours off you just make them mad. But Kendra and Ana still don't return your calls do they?

But after I hit SEND, I sit there and wonder if maybe, just maybe, he's right. Bringing up my dad on the first date . . . was it too much? Serafina didn't seem to mind. She even seemed to understand. But still. Anyway, I better try to keep the conversation lighter tonight. Dead parents are not exactly lively party talk.

I open up the e-mail from my remaining parent.

To: justinb597@webmail.com
From: Lblakewell@walkerandco.com
Subject: Amazing

Honey—
The date with Neil (that's his name) went really, really well. Don't worry, I won't embarrass you with details. But this might be something good.
love,
Mom

Neil. What kind of a stupid, square, boring name is that? The minute I'm out of the house she's hooking up with some guy named *Neil*. It's like she was just waiting until I was finally out of the way. By the time I get home she'll probably be telling me how *Neil* is stepfather material.

I close the e-mail without replying. Anyway, Mrs. B said she'd give me a ride downtown when she takes Aspen to meet some friends of hers for lunch, and she's already calling to me that it's time to go.

Chapter 13

MRS. B DROPS ME OFF ON MAIN STREET. Except for dinner at Jack's Shack with Serafina, this is the first time I've been on my own in the Hamptons, without a little kid hanging on to me.

There's a coffee place on the corner. I ask for the thing with the longest name on their menu board. It turns out to be half a cup of coffee with milk and whipped cream, drizzled over the top with chocolate and caramel. It's like an ice cream sundae with coffee underneath. I don't even have to add sugar.

It cost five dollars. Back home you can get coffee for a dollar fifty at the deli, and it comes with a bagel too. But who cares? I even drop fifty cents in the tip jar before I take my coffee-dessert outside, over to a little round table near the sidewalk.

A tall, skinny woman with dark hair walks by, wearing a denim jacket with a rose embroidered on the back. I swear I've seen her on TV somewhere. I'm trying hard to look cool, trying not to sit here grinning like an idiot, but I have to admit, it's hard. I'm sitting here, sipping my five-dollar coffee, in the Hamptons. I'm going to a party tonight with a beautiful girl. A beautiful *rich* girl. And nobody looking at me can tell I'm just the hired help. I look like I belong.

After I finish up my coffee, I take a stroll down Main Street. I look into the window of an art gallery. They've got stuff in there that could make Mrs. B's exploding eggplant painting look good. I wander into a bookstore and read the backs of a few books. Then I stop in front of a place that sells clothes.

Shirts, chinos, jeans, tossed around casually behind the big display window, lying over packing crates like they're no big deal. No price tags are visible, just to point out that the people who shop here don't have to think about how much something costs.

There, in the corner, is the perfect shirt. I think I've been looking for this shirt all my life. Short sleeves, gunmetal gray, with skinny stripes in a gray that's just one or two shades darker. It's not shiny, but something about the way the fabric hangs tells me it's silk. I know if I could touch it, it would be thin and smooth but feel heavy, a lot of weight to it. This is not a shirt that shouts class. It whispers it. That's the point, of course. Real class doesn't have to shout.

I can't afford it. I'm pretty sure I can't afford to walk in that shop and breathe.

But hey, I don't *know* that, right? The price tag's not on there. Maybe it's on sale or something.

No harm in going in to look.

The air in the shop is so air-conditioned it gives me goose bumps. The lady behind the counter is wearing a tight mint-green sweater. She smiles at me.

There are only about three racks of clothes. I find the shirt easily. It feels between my fingers just the way I thought it would.

"Excuse me." It's ridiculous how nervous I am. It's not like this lady can tell just by looking at me that I don't have any money. For all she knows I'm a real customer. I clear my throat. "Can I try this on?"

She smiles again and points me toward the dressing room.

The material feels absolutely smooth, like cool water, against my skin. I do the buttons up carefully and check myself out in the mirror.

Oh, yeah.

This is *my* shirt. This shirt has been waiting for me to come along. I need to walk into Carter's party tonight wearing this shirt.

I look at the price tag.

It's stupid to be disappointed. I knew I couldn't afford it. I knew that all along. I put the shirt on its hanger and carry it back into the shop. I'm about to hang it up on the rack when I spot the little sign on the counter.

IF FOR ANY REASON YOU ARE NOT COMPLETELY SATISFIED WITH YOUR PURCHASE, WE WILL BE HAPPY TO GIVE YOU A FULL REFUND. PLEASE RETAIN YOUR RECEIPT.

And I hear my mom's voice.

The bills will come to me, and if I see any charges on here for CDs or computer games or clothes . . . especially *clothes, Justin . . .*

But if I return the shirt tomorrow, she wouldn't just see the charge. She'd see a credit also. It would come out to zero. No harm, no foul, right?

I already know my mom would not like me doing this. But I'm digging my wallet out of my pocket anyway. I'll deal with my mom later, when I get back home. Who knows, maybe she'll be so caught up with this guy Neil she's dating that she won't even notice. And anyway, whatever else happens, I'll show up at Carter's party looking like I belong there.

Liz was right when she said that all this place needed was a drawbridge and a moat. Castle Carter is right on the water, only about five blocks from the Beltons' place. There are cars in the driveway and up and down the street, just like I thought there would be.

Serafina and I agreed to meet up at the party. I'm not crazy about this. If we don't walk in together, we didn't really come together, and that makes it less of a date. It also makes it less clear to every other guy in the place that she's with me.

But since she's driving and I'm walking, the only other alternative was to let *her* pick *me* up. And that's just not how the script should go.

I'm wondering how many gardeners Carter's folks employ to keep their front lawn looking like this. There's a brick path between bushes with bunches of weird, electric blue flowers. Little lights are shining on the bricks so you don't trip and accidentally scuff your shoes. I'm about to ring the bell when I notice that the door is open an inch or two, so I give it a little shove and look in.

A big room with wide plate-glass windows that I guess, during the day, would give you a view of water and sand. Now all you can see is a pool with a light glimmering an eerie greenish blue under the smooth water. Inside, the lights are mostly off and music is pounding. Even though it's summer, the air drifting in off the ocean is chilly, and there's a fire in the fireplace. You could probably roast a whole pig in there if you wanted to. On one side of the room kids are dancing, the girls in short skirts and clingy tops, the guys mostly in T-shirts and shorts. I spot Kath with the red hair, wearing a green dress that doesn't cover much more than her bathing suit did at the pool.

I rub the collar of my new shirt between my fingers. It's my good luck charm, my passport. Feeling the thin, slick cloth between my fingers relaxes me a little. It reminds me that someday I won't *need* a passport. Someday I'll walk up to a house like this and I won't be nervous, because I'll *own* it. It'll be mine.

Right now, though, I'll confess to being just a little bit jumpy.

"Hey, look, it's Mr. Doubtfire. The boy nanny."

And a greeting like that from Carter doesn't help to reassure me.

"Just *kidding,* man!" He's laughing at me. "Lighten up, glad you're here, you want a drink?"

"Yeah, thanks." What I really want is to ditch him and look for Serafina, but he *is* the guy throwing the party, after all. And maybe he didn't mean anything with that Mr. Doubtfire crack. He's being friendly enough now, leading me over to a bar set into the wall, wineglasses hanging down from a rack above.

"What do you want?" he asks me. "My dad brought back some really great sake from his last trip to Japan. He'll never miss one bottle."

Sake? Is he serious? Most of the parties I've been to, a few of the guys just sneak in a six-pack or two, and that's about it. "Just a beer," I say—suavely, I hope. Like I'm really bored with sake.

"Imported? There's some Belgian ale in here," he says, digging around in a cooler full of ice.

"Yeah, sure." He hands me a bottle, dripping ice water, and I try to twist the cap off. It doesn't twist. I try harder. There's no way I'm looking like a weakling in front of Carter. The metal ridges on the cap bite deeply into my fingers. I don't mean to, but I let out a little grunt.

"Here." Carter holds out a bottle opener. "This kind doesn't twist off."

Oh.

"So," I say, after swallowing a long, cold mouthful. Hey, those Belgians really know how to make beer. "Is Serafina here yet?"

"She didn't come with you?"

I don't miss the look he gives me, a little too interested. Suddenly I don't like this guy. I don't care if I'm in his house, at his party, drinking his imported beer. I just don't like him at all.

"No, we were going to meet up here." I keep myself from adding anything lame, like "She had something to do in town," or "I was too busy squeezing my zits to pick her up." I don't owe this guy any explanations.

"Really. Haven't seen her yet. No, wait—there she is."

Serafina's just coming in the front door.

Funny how, even though there's not much light in the room, most of it seems focused on her. She has on this dark red dress that brushes against her when she walks. And she's walking right over here, to me.

Or maybe to Carter. He's standing here too. When she gets here, I can't really tell which of us she's smiling at.

"Hello, Justin."

There, see? She said my name first.

"Carter, this is a very nice party."

Hmmm. But she said more words to him.

Before I can even say hello, Carter's already talking.

"Hey, Fina, glad you could make it. Look at you, all that *and* a bag of chips." He looks her up and down like he's hungry and she's a slice of pizza. And what's with that fake rap star talk? Some rich Hamptons white boy pretending he's from the 'hood. Give me a break.

Apparently I'm not the only one who's not thrilled with the way Carter's eyeing Serafina, because a girl suddenly materializes at his side. She's got hair that looks like she slept on it, lots of mascara around her eyes, and lipstick so dark it's almost black. It takes me a few seconds to recognize her as Autumn, one of the girls I met when I was with Serafina at Jack's.

"Carter?" she says, looking up at him. Even though her hair adds about three inches to her height, she still doesn't come up to his chin. "Let's dance, okay?"

"In a minute."

"But—"

"I'm getting Serafina something to drink, Autumn," Carter says. "Listen, could you get some more chips out of the kitchen?"

She goes, but she's not happy about it.

"Diet Coke," Serafina says when Carter asks what she wants. She takes the cup he hands her and turns back to me.

"When did you get here?"

"Just now. I mean, a few minutes ago. Right before you did, actually." Good grief, how long can I take to answer one simple question?

"That's good. That you weren't waiting long."

Slightly awkward pause. Apparently we've exhausted the conversational possibilities of my arrival time.

"That little boy, Aspen? He was all right after the beach?"

Oh yeah. The last time she saw Aspen I looked like a child abuser. Time to mend that little piece of my reputation.

"Oh, sure." I laugh. "He was mostly just tired, I think. There was this dog . . ."

"Justin is a nanny for a little boy," Serafina explains, turning to Carter. Right, like he's going to have forgotten this.

"Yeah, and he loves dogs," I say. "So what happened—"

"Uh-huh." Somehow, without actually being rude, Carter manages to convey the idea that nothing is more boring than standing around talking about little kids. "Hey, I have to go say hi to some more people. See you later, Fina." He touches her lightly on the arm and moves off to greet some new arrivals at the door.

I know that move, touching a girl like that to say good-bye. That's a Dillon move. It's definitely not a move you pull on another guy's date. Does he think I won't notice?

"It's a good party, isn't it?" Serafina says.

More likely he thinks I won't do anything about it, here at his own party. He's pretty much right about that, I guess. Wait, Serafina just said something. *Pay attention when she talks,* Liz told me. The first rule of good dating, and I'm already blowing it.

"What? Yeah, great party. Now, I mean."

"Now? Why now?"

"Well, it's a lot better than it was before you got here."

It's so cool watching her blush.

"Do you want to get something to eat?" I inquire.

"Sure." She's got great dimples when she smiles. "Oh, wait—" Her head goes up like somebody just called her name. "I love this song. Dance with me?"

You've probably already guessed that I was lying when I told Liz I could dance.

I mean, I *can* dance. In theory. Wiggle your hips, move your feet, swing your arms, yeah, sure. It's doing all that stuff *at the same time* that I have a problem with. And doing it to music. When I got put together on the assembly line, the guy in charge of rhythm was off somewhere on a cigarette break.

Serafina's bouncing a little on her toes in time to the music, her eyes wide, her smile eager. How can I possibly tell her I can't dance?

On the other hand, how can I possibly get out there and flap around like a chicken in front of a party full of rich kids? Particularly when one of them has the hots for the girl I'm trying so hard to impress?

I open my mouth, not at all sure about what's going to come out.

"Chips?"

Carter pops up at Serafina's elbow, holding a big bowl of weird blue tortilla chips in one hand and a little bowl of bright red salsa in the other.

"Oh, thank you." Serafina scoops up some salsa in a chip

and pops it into her mouth. "We're just going to dance. Justin?"

I can't do it. I just can't tell her I can't dance. I take a step toward her.

Just as I move forward, intending to walk past Carter toward the dance floor, somebody behind Carter pushes him a little. At least, that's what it looks like, because he stumbles forward a step. The bowl in his right hand tilts, threatening to spill tortilla chips all over the carpet. He grabs for it with his left hand, apparently forgetting one small fact: his left hand is already holding a bowl of salsa.

The salsa bowl flips over slowly in midair.

A second later, the bowl is upside down on the carpet. There's not that much salsa left to spill, though, because most of it is plastered over the front of my new shirt.

"Oh no!" Serafina's dabbing uselessly at the mess on my shirt with the tips of her fingers. "Oh, Justin, oh, that's too bad. Oh, I'm sorry."

"Yeah, man, I'm really sorry," Carter says. I think he's smirking a little, but maybe I'm wrong. After he bends down to pick up the salsa bowl off the floor, he honestly looks like he feels bad. "I've got to get some paper towels before people walk in that. My mom will freak. Sorry about the shirt, really."

I'm about to start yelling. I'm about to start using words I bet these trust fund, private school, Upper East Side kids have never even heard. My *shirt*. My new shirt, the perfect shirt, the one that makes me look like I belong here.

The shirt I was going to return to the store tomorrow.

But I can't get a word out. I can't say a thing. What am

I supposed to do, tell all these kids—tell Carter—tell *Serafina*—that I can't actually afford the shirt I'm wearing?

"Come into the kitchen," Serafina says, tugging on my arm. "We should rinse that off right away. Maybe it will come out."

I let her pull me into the kitchen. She grabs a handful of paper towel, runs water on them, and starts scrubbing away at the front of my shirt.

She's close to me, her head bent down, so I can smell that strawberry shampoo, even stronger than the spicy tomato smell of the salsa.

"Oh, Justin, I don't know. I'm afraid it won't come out." She looks up at me.

This time I don't hesitate. I just lean down a little. Her face tips back, and one of her hands comes up to touch my cheek, turning my head a little to one side.

Her lips are warm. Her mouth tastes a little bit like salsa. I put my hands on her waist, and she lets me pull her in a little closer. I think she comes up on her tiptoes, because suddenly I don't have to bend down so far to get my lips to meet hers.

When I open my eyes and pull back to take a breath, she's smiling. Over her shoulder I can see Carter, standing in the kitchen door with a wad of bunched-up paper towels in his hand. Now he doesn't look sorry anymore. He looks like he'd love to have me turning slowly on a spit over the fire in his great big fireplace.

I bend my head down to kiss Serafina again.

Chapter 14

I DON'T GET BACK to the Beltons' until after two o'clock. The next morning even an ice-cold shower and two cups of coffee (that's ten spoonfuls of sugar, in case you're counting) aren't really enough to get my eyes all the way open.

A phone call is, though.

"A young lady," Mrs. B says, handing me the phone and giving me a look at the same time. I really hate that look adults get—that smug one that says "I know everything you're going through because I've been there myself, but I won't tell you what will happen because that would spoil all the fun." News flash—you haven't been here. This is my life, not yours.

But I'm too excited at the moment to get really annoyed. I grab the phone. "Hi, Serafina?"

"No, sorry," the voice on the other end of the phone says. "Just Liz."

Liz is taking Max to the park this afternoon, and she wants to know if Aspen and I can meet them there. I wish I could ask if Serafina will come too, but Mrs. B's right there in the kitchen, cleaning up the breakfast dishes, and I don't feel like going into details in front of her. So I just agree to meet Liz at the park after lunch and hang up.

Serafina will probably be there. She's friends with Liz, they hang out together all the time. Yeah. She should be there.

And even if she's not, I can probably see her tonight. Or tomorrow night at least. I guess I should have set something up when we left Carter's party last night. But I was too excited, knowing I was going to get the chance to kiss her again.

That was pretty much the highlight of the party, kissing Serafina once by her car to say good-bye, and twice in the kitchen with Carter looking on. Showing him in no uncertain terms whose girl Serafina is.

After I kissed her the second time in the kitchen, Serafina pulled back a little. Not like she was mad or anything. Just like she wanted a little breathing space.

"We should get back to the party, I think," she said. "No one will notice your shirt."

No one could fail to notice my shirt, is the truth. But I followed her back out into the living room, where I finally came clean and confessed that I can't dance. I thought maybe we'd go out back, sit next to the pool, dangle our feet in the water, kiss some more. But instead, Serafina danced with her girlfriends. I leaned against the wall and watched.

A few people came by and talked to me. I told them the red stain on my shirt was from a bullet wound but that it wasn't life-threatening. I drank another beer. Then I switched to Coke so I wouldn't break Liz's rule and get drunk and bore Serafina.

I started to wonder why there wasn't anything in Liz's rules about *me* getting bored.

But none of that mattered when I got to walk Serafina out to her car and kiss her good night. And none of it's going to matter when I see her again.

After lunch, when Aspen and I get to the park, I pull my bike helmet off and run my hands through my hair even before I get Aspen down from the kiddie seat. But it's all wasted. Looking around, I see Liz orchestrating a game of tag between Max and two girls who look a little bit older, but no sign of Serafina.

"She's on some boat trip with the family she works for," Liz says when I ask. "She'll be gone all day. Didn't she tell you?" When I shake my head, she smirks and says, "Guess she must have had something else on her mind."

"The McGraws adopt some more kids?" I ask, to get her off this subject, looking at the two girls running around with Max.

"My sisters," Liz says. "Annie and Ellie." The girls look exactly the same age. They must be twins but not identical ones. Annie has freckles and blonde braids the same color as Liz's; Ellie's got short brown curls and is missing a front tooth. "Usually one of the neighbors watches them during the day," Liz explains. "But she's got the flu, so I have to keep an eye on them until my dad finishes up the job he's on."

"What about your mom?"

"She's not around." Liz says it a little shortly. No trespassers. I get the message. "Look, don't say anything about my sisters to the people you work for, okay? I don't want the McGraws to know. They probably wouldn't like it."

"Yeah, sure."

"You're it!" Annie shrieks.

"No, you're it!" Ellie yells back.

"You!"

"No, you!"

Liz goes over to break it up before somebody gets killed. Aspen's sticking close to my side, but he's looking over at the game kind of hopefully.

"Want to play tag?" I ask him. He puts his index finger in the corner of his mouth and nods.

"C'mon, it'll be fun."

I lead him over to where Liz is saying, "First Ellie's it, then Annie. No, I mean it, if you guys start arguing there's going to be no more tag. You promised you'd be good today."

"Tell you what," I say. "*I'll* be it. Ready? And I'm going to catch *you* first! Yaaaaargh!" I make a dash at Ellie. Of course I miss, but she dances out of the way, giggling and screaming.

When the game of tag winds down, we herd the kids over to the sandbox and collapse on a bench nearby.

"Fun party last night?" Liz asks.

"Definitely." I don't feel like going into details, though, so I come up with something to distract her. "Hey, you still have my sunglasses, you know."

"Oh, duh. I'm sorry, I meant to bring them with me."

"No big deal."

"Tomorrow's my day off. I could drop them by your place."

"Really, don't worry about it." I just brought it up so we could get off the subject of the party. Liz may be my spy, but she's still a girl. I'm not about to discuss kissing techniques with her.

"Just tell me where you live, okay?" I give up and tell her. This girl is persistent. "I'll come by," she promises.

Meanwhile, Annie and Ellie are bickering over who gets to put a flag made out of a Skittles wrapper on the top of their castle. Max and Aspen watch silently, a little awed by the presence of two older women. Liz sighs. "You know how you always read about twins who are a little telepathic, can feel each other's pain, that sort of thing? I wish ours were that kind. Hey, you two, knock it off!"

A car honks from the street, a beat-up old Chevy, and a hand waves out the window. Liz looks up, frowning. "That looks like Mel's car, but my dad was supposed to pick the girls up." The Chevy squeezes into a parking space next to a red convertible, and a skinny blonde woman gets out, her hair piled up on the top of her head, her skirt short and tight.

"Ellie, Annie, let's go!" Liz dusts sand off her sisters' shorts. "Justin, can you keep an eye on Max for a minute?"

"Sure, no problem." I watch as Ellie and Annie run across the park to get hugged by the blonde woman. Liz follows behind them and gets a kiss on the cheek. Who is this woman? Not the mom, obviously, since Liz said she's not in the picture. Aunt? Neighbor? Friend?

Aspen and Max and I have started on the moat to the castle when Liz comes back, minus her sisters.

"My dad got stuck somewhere on a job," she says, sitting down in the sand. "A pipe broke or something. So Mel's going to take the girls for the afternoon."

"Who's Mel?"

"My dad's girlfriend."

I look over at her in surprise. She seems so casual about it. *My dad's girlfriend.* Like it's no big deal.

"You like her?"

"Sure, she's okay." Liz shrugs. "I mean, she's always bugging me to wear lipstick, and she keeps trying to put highlights in my hair or dye it red or something. But she's fun, and she likes the girls."

"You don't need highlights." I have no idea why I said that. I mean, it's true—Liz's hair is her best feature, very light blonde, almost silvery, and kind of shiny in the sun. But I'm not really thinking about that. I'm thinking about my mom's e-mail, about that guy from her work. I'm still thinking about it when an ice cream truck pulls up in the parking space that Mel just left, tinkling that annoying little tune.

"Max's dad gave me some money for ice cream," Liz says. "Is that okay for Aspen?"

"I want chocolate!" Aspen shouts.

"I guess it better be," I say as Aspen gets a grip on my hand and drags me over to the curb, nearly dislocating my shoulder in the process.

Aspen and I both get chocolate, mine in a cone, his in a cup with sprinkles. Liz gets peppermint.

"Max, honey, what do you want?" Liz asks him.

Max's face is screwed up with the effort of serious thought.

"This'll take a while," Liz says, with a sigh. There are some benches along the sidewalk. Aspen and I go to sit there and eat our ice cream while Max makes up his mind.

Aspen practically sticks his nose in his cup to go after the last few sprinkles. I'm mopping up his face when I hear a voice.

"Isn't that sweet."

Three guesses who. I can't believe I didn't recognize the car. The ice-cream truck's parked right next to it.

"C'mon, Carter."

That's Autumn, putting a hand on Carter's arm. Today she's in preppy mode rather than goth, with khaki shorts and a plaid sleeveless shirt.

Carter ignores her. "Hey, too bad about your shirt last night," he says to me. "I wanted to tell you, I'd be glad to pay for the dry cleaning. Since being a nanny probably doesn't get you all that much money."

It might even have been a nice thing to say. Except for his voice. And his face. Even Autumn, who frankly doesn't seem all that bright, gets the idea that something's wrong. She pulls her hand back from Carter's arm and moves a step away.

"Accidents happen," I say, not getting up. "Great party last night. Too bad Serafina and I couldn't stay longer."

I make it sound like I went home with Serafina instead of just walking her to her car. After all, how does Carter know I didn't?

He keeps smiling. "Ah, that doesn't matter," he says. "Sometimes girls like to hang out with other girls. But they always come back to a man after a while."

Carter's about three inches taller than I am. Standing up isn't going to give me much of an advantage. I drop my ice cream cone on the bench and do it anyway.

Generally I try to avoid getting into fights. Not only do you risk getting hurt, but you also look really stupid doing it. Have you ever watched a couple of guys throwing punches? They look like idiots, rolling around in the dirt.

You come out a lot better, not to mention on the right side of authorities like principals and police officers, if you say something vicious and brilliant and then walk calmly away.

The trouble is, it's hard to think of something vicious and brilliant when all you really want to do is smash somebody's face in.

"Oops!" says a very innocent voice from behind Carter's back. "That's your car, isn't it? I'm really sorry."

Liz is standing next to the red convertible, holding an empty ice-cream cone. She has Max's hand in hers.

"Can you get an ice-cream stain out of leather?" she asks.

"You . . ." Carter's face goes from alarmed to furious. "What did you do?" He hurries over to his car to check out the damage.

Liz drops her empty cone on the ground. She reaches over and picks up my chocolate cone from where it's lying on its side on the bench. It's pretty much liquid by now.

"Is it bad? I'm sorry, it just fell right off the cone." She comes over to stand next to Carter, inspecting the cream-colored leather seat. "Oh, look, it fell right there." She points with the hand holding what's left of my cone. Chocolate drips off her fingers.

"Watch out!"

"For what? Oh, no, look at that." She brings her hand to her mouth and licks off chocolate. "Dry-cleaning leather is so expensive, isn't it?"

"You knew that was my car. You did that on purpose, you little . . ." Carter's mouth works. He can't figure out what to call her.

"Hey, don't call people names in front of a little kid," Liz says sternly. "You don't want to teach him bad habits, do you? C'mon, Max, honey. Sit down and finish your ice cream."

Autumn runs over to the ice-cream truck and comes back with paper napkins. Carter ignores her.

Liz and Max sit down next to Aspen. She makes a big fuss over helping him with his ice cream. Looks like he got vanilla, after all that effort.

"Let's go," Carter says angrily. Autumn gets into the convertible with him. Carter slams the door and drives off. I wave.

Liz watches them go, looking satisfied.

"You owe me an ice-cream cone," she says.

I get her one. Double dip.

Chapter 15

WHEN I GET DOWNSTAIRS ON SUNDAY MORNING, Mr. B is in the middle of making pancakes, standing by the griddle with a spatula in his hand. Judging from the intense look on his face, the whole kitchen could go critical if he doesn't flip the pancakes at just the right moment. Mrs. B has removed herself from the scene, sipping her coffee out on the back deck.

Since it looks like breakfast will take a while, I wander into the den to check my e-mail. Bonanza. One from Alex, one from Dillon, one from my mom.

Dillon's e-mail doesn't take long to read.

To: justinb597@webmail.com
From: playboy311@netwave.com
Subject: Re: re: watch out

so what? plenty other fish
just saying liten up

Alex, on the other hand, doesn't sound like lightening up is in the cards.

To: justinb597@webmail.com
From: alxskywlkr@webmail.com

You know how you're always telling me I have to talk abt the things girls are interested in and I tell you I can't sustain a conversation abt Britney Spears and belly button rings? But Claire's into the same stuff I am like Mac vs pc and why everything shld run on Linux.

Oh, listen to this. Geek true love.

She lives in Hoboken too. Maybe I can see her on some of these weekends of torture with my dad.

I scanned in this pix of her. But she's better looking in real life.

Frizzy hair, half-inch glasses, bad skin. That's what I'm expecting. What I'm not prepared for is . . . a hottie. The red hair curls, but it's not frizzy. Nice eyes. Nice smile.

I'm still slightly baffled by the concept of Alex with a good-looking girlfriend as I open up my mom's e-mail.

To: justinb597@webmail.com
From: Lblakewell@walkerandco.com
Subject: How's Everything?

Honey—
Haven't heard from you in a few days. Hope that means you're busy and having a good time. Neil and I saw a movie

last night—the kind of chick flick you won't go to see with me. He must be trying hard to make a good impression, huh? I think you'll like him a lot when you meet him.

love,

Mom

Now she wants me to meet him? So she wants to spend all her time with some loser, that's her business. But why does it mean I have to hang out with him too?

"Justin!" Mr. B yells from the kitchen. "Pancakes! Get 'em while they're hot!"

I close my mom's e-mail and hurry to the kitchen.

It turns out that Mr. and Mrs. B got an invitation from some friends to play golf at this big fancy club. As they're packing up golf clubs after breakfast, Mr. B looks out into the backyard and frowns.

"Justin," he says. "Those bushes are looking a little thirsty."

I look over at the bushes with the pink flowers that we planted a few days ago. They look okay to me, but then, I don't have much experience with gardening. There's not much you can plant in a one-bedroom apartment on the ninth floor.

"Can you put the hose under them and turn on a little trickle of water? Let it run all morning. They'll soak it up. Oh, and here."

He pulls out his wallet and gives me a handful of bills.

Maybe I look a little surprised, because he smiles. "For your first week," he says. "Coming, dear!"

He hefts the golf clubs up over his shoulder and heads out the door, leaving me looking down at the money in my hand.

I mean, it's not like I didn't know they were going to pay me. I knew that. I even knew how *much* they were going to pay me.

But I've never actually held one hundred and fifty dollars, in cash, in my hands before.

Andrew Jackson looks up sternly at me from the neat, crisp twenties. Seven of them. And one ten.

It's going to take five of these twenties to pay my mom back for the shirt that Carter ruined. But still. That's not until I get home again. And I've got this money right now.

"Justin!" Aspen tugs at my shirt. "I wanna play. I wanna play action heroes."

"Hang on a minute," I tell him. The phone book's over on the kitchen counter. I flip it open to "Restaurants." There's Antonio's, right on the front page.

I make a reservation for tomorrow night. Then I set the hose running under the bushes, like Mr. B told me to. Then I discuss the morning's program with Aspen. I try to talk him into the beach, the pool, the park, or anywhere I might have a chance of running into Serafina, but he's not buying it. All he wants to do is stay home and play with his action figures.

He takes the firefighter, the policeman, and the Navy SEAL. After some consideration he gives me the mountain climber. What am I supposed to do with a mountain climber?

I make him climb up the leg of the coffee table a few times. Then I sit around watching Aspen's plastic heroes beat up a fuzzy green dinosaur. "You're a bad guy," the SEAL says to the dinosaur before kicking it in the head.

This goes on for a while.

I try to sneak a magazine off the coffee table and read it, but Aspen's on to me.

"Play," he says. "You have to play."

Right. I have to play. I'm getting paid to play.

I heave a sigh of relief when lunchtime rolls around. Even making a PB&J sandwich is more exciting than this.

We eat out on the back deck, with Yippy and Yappy making a racket on the other side of the fence. Aspen is painstakingly unscrewing the top cookie on his Oreo when the doorbell rings.

"I'll be right back," I say to Aspen. "Hang out a minute."

Later on I realize that I must have forgotten to close the sliding door behind me.

Liz is at the front door, holding my sunglasses in her hand. Ecstasy. Someone over the age of four to talk to.

"Thanks." I slip the sunglasses into my pocket. "Come on in."

She hesitates. "You're probably having lunch or something."

"Certainly. I can offer you the specialty of the house, crushed peanuts and mashed strawberries on freshly sliced whole-grain bread," I say, holding the door and waving her in like a maître d'. "With a glass of chilled cow's milk and our elegant chocolate cookies with a creamy center to round off the meal."

She grins. "Okay." She steps in, drops her backpack on a table, and looks at something behind me. "What a cute dog. It looks like it got in a mud puddle, though."

Dog?

I turn around. There, in the hall, looking up at us and whapping its tail back and forth with general happiness, is

Yippy. Or maybe it's Yappy. One of the little white fuzz balls from next door. Except this one is no longer white. It's covered from nose to tail with dripping mud.

The tail swings back and forth. Little droplets of mud splatter on the walls.

"All right," I say very calmly. "I'm going to get behind it. And if I miss it, you grab it."

"Yes, sir, at once, sir."

I'll explain to her later how this isn't a joke. Carefully I make a wide circle around Yappy, who just stands there, dripping. Moving slowly, silently, I get behind the little beast, lean over, and pounce. Gotcha! Yappy squirms around in my hands and tries to lick my face, but I hold him out at arm's length. Okay, it's not so bad. It's just mud on the hall floor, which is wood. It's not like the little mutt got on the expensive rugs and the white couch in the living room all dirty.

Liz starts to laugh. "You don't like dogs, huh?"

"I like dogs," I say grimly. "I don't like animated wigs." Especially when they're muddy and in my employer's house. How did the animal get inside anyway? And how did it get so dirty? Holding the sticky, wiggling, yelping dog out in front of me, I stalk toward the back deck. There I see Aspen, kneeling next to the new flower bushes right where the hose is running, feeding Yippy the rest of his Oreos. Yippy's obviously been digging and rolling in the gloppy mud, just like Yappy.

"Aspen!" I yell. "What are you doing?"

"He likes me!" Aspen exclaims joyfully.

Yippy flings herself on Aspen and starts licking his face. He collapses onto his back in giggles, and the dog jumps on top of him, decorating his T-shirt with muddy paw prints.

Yappy wants to join in the fun. Suddenly it's like trying to keep a grip on a wet, slippery tornado. The next thing I know I'm holding on to the dog by one back leg. He yelps. I'm so scared that I'm hurting him, I drop him, nose first. Somehow he lands on all four paws and dashes off to jump on Aspen.

Aspen and the dogs are having the time of their lives.

"Enough!" I say, jumping down the stairs three at a time and landing in the yard. I get one hand on Yappy's collar and the other under Yippy's stomach. "Aspen, you know you're not supposed to play with—"

Yippy bounces straight up into the air, out of my hand, runs between my legs, and takes off for the open back door.

Liz lunges for her and misses.

I fall over right on top of Aspen. I catch myself with one hand so I don't squash him into a pancake, but I lose my hold on Yappy's collar.

"Catch him!" I yell at Liz.

She tries, she really does, but I swear that little dog's got some greyhound in him.

"Catch him, catch him!" Aspen hollers and runs after the dogs into the house.

Liz and I run after Aspen.

Yappy skids across the kitchen floor, leaving long muddy streaks. "I'll get him!" Liz yells. "You get the other one!"

She's trying to corner Yappy between the dishwasher and the sink.

I take off for the living room.

Yippy's dancing around on, of course, the white couch. Aspen makes a running leap and lands facedown beside her.

"Aspen, get off of there!" I holler. Aspen's about as muddy as the dog.

The kid isn't really trying to grab Yippy. He's just delirious with the excitement. Yippy squirts out between his hands and makes a flying leap, heading straight for . . .

. . . oh, *shit* . . .

. . . the coffee table and Mrs. B's *Exploding Purple Eggplant Sonata #4.*

Yippy lands on some magazines and skates across the glass tabletop like she's on ice.

I lunge forward, crack my shin on a corner of the table, say a few words mannies are definitely not supposed to say, and get my hands on the painting, snatching it up two seconds before Yippy plants her wet, muddy paws right where it had been.

If I hadn't broken my leg on the coffee table and if I didn't have my hands full of an ugly, expensive piece of art, I could probably keep my balance. But as it is, I just end up hopping a few steps before I fall on my butt.

Yippy, meanwhile, sails right off the edge of the coffee table and lands on Aspen's action figures. A second later she's off again, with the Navy SEAL in her mouth.

"No, no!" Aspen wails. "*Bad* dog!"

Now he actually wants to catch her, but he's seriously out-classed. All he can do is run behind Yippy, which only makes her go faster. Rugs slide across the slippery wood floor.

I stagger to my feet, set the painting on the mantel for safety, and join the chase, even disabled as I am.

Yippy dives under the couch. We can hear crunching noises.

"She's eating him!" Aspen sobs.

I lie down flat and make a swipe under the couch, but I can't quite reach the dog. Okay, we'll have to move the couch. I stand up and grab one of the arms.

"Hold on," Liz says.

She's standing in the living room doorway, with a couple of muddy paw prints on her shorts. She's got something in her hand.

It's the crust from Aspen's sandwich.

She kneels down in front of the couch and holds out the bit of peanut-butter-smeared bread. After a minute Yippy's little black nose pokes out. Liz gives her a tiny bite of the crust and then holds the rest about a foot away from her. Yippy trots happily out, scarfs up the treat, and lets Liz pick her up with no trouble.

I stand on one foot, rubbing my shin.

Aspen wiggles under the couch to get his Navy SEAL back from hazardous duty.

The living room is a disaster. Dirty footprints all over the floor. The couch is no longer white. And Aspen looks like he lost a mud-wrestling tournament. Well, at least I saved the painting.

Was I thinking just a few hours ago that being a manny was boring?

We take Yippy outside. Yappy's on the deck, one end of a dishtowel tied to his collar and the other end to a leg of the table. Liz is pretty resourceful, I have to give her that. The gate between the Beltons' yard and the neighbors' is open.

"Aspen," I say sternly. "Did you let those dogs in here?"

Aspen clutches his SEAL in both hands and scowls at the ground.

"I just wanted to *play* with them." He sighs, like I'm the most unreasonable manny in the world.

He deserved to have his SEAL chewed up. I'm tempted to start munching on the rest of those action figures myself, just to teach him a lesson.

I'm even more tempted when I hear a car pulling up in the driveway.

We throw the dogs back into their own yard and latch the gate. I wonder what the neighbors will say when they see them, but at the moment I've got more pressing problems.

"I better go," Liz says, looking alarmed.

"You don't have to—"

"You supposed to have guests when you're working?"

Shit. No, I guess not. I mean, it's not like I invited her over or anything. But it's going to be pretty easy for the Beltons to believe that I didn't have an eye on Aspen because I was talking with Liz.

Which I guess, now that I'm thinking about it, might be true.

But there's a drawback to Liz's plan. "There's no side gate," I tell her. The only way out of the Beltons' backyard is through the house. I get Aspen by the hand, Liz follows, and the three of us walk into the front hall just as the Beltons are opening the door.

Mrs. B stops to look, first at Liz, then at me, and then at the devastation wrought in her living room. Mr. B, coming up behind her with one bag of golf clubs in his hand and the other one over his shoulder, stops to look too.

Mrs. B's expression doesn't change, but she lifts her eyebrows slightly.

"Justin?" she asks politely. "What, exactly, happened here?"

Chapter
16

IN THE APPROXIMATELY THREE MINUTES that have passed since I heard the Beltons' car pull up, I've been working on a calm, reasonable explanation of why their living room looks like it got hit with a flood combined with a hurricane. So I don't know why all these words are coming out of my mouth in such a mess. "It was the dogs. From next door. Yippy and Yappy. Aspen opened the gate. And this is Liz. She came by—"

"Just to return Justin's sunglasses," Liz says nervously. "He didn't ask me over or anything."

"But I went to answer the doorbell, and Aspen, I guess, while I was gone, he opened the gate, he wanted to play with the dogs—"

"*Bad* dogs!"

"And I guess I sort of left the back door . . . open, I guess . . ." My explanation loses steam and trails to a halt.

"All right," Mr. B says, and lowers the golf clubs to the ground. "Could we have that again, a little more slowly, please?"

I run through everything again, this time in full sentences.

Mr. B nods and looks at the living room. Mrs. B keeps her eyes on me.

"Well," says Mr. B when I'm done. "Looks like you and Aspen have some cleaning up to do."

And that's it. I heave a silent sigh of relief. I was afraid the dry cleaning bills for the couch cushions were going to come out of my salary. After the shirt fiasco at Carter's party, I really can't afford any more financial reversals.

"I'll help," Liz offers.

"No, thank you. Liz, is it? You're a nanny too?" Liz nods. She has her hands in her pockets, her fists bunched up. "You should probably get back to work, don't you think?" Mrs. B says to her. "Justin, come into the kitchen for a minute, please."

And while Liz looks around for her backpack, I follow Mrs. B into the kitchen.

"Justin," she says. "We hired you to look after Aspen. When you're working, that's not socializing time."

"I know," I say, a little irritated. Liz already *said* that she only came over to return my sunglasses. "I didn't ask her over here. We weren't hanging out or anything." I kind of skip the part about how I invited her in for lunch.

Mrs. B looks a little suspicious. "Liz is a very pretty girl," she says.

Huh?

"But your focus has to be on Aspen while you're working."

Why is it that adults never think you understand something until they've said it three times? "I know," I say again.

"On your time off, that's fine. I know you and Liz went to a party on Friday—"

"Me and *Liz*?" I think my voice gets a little louder than I realized. "No way. I'm not *dating* Liz! She's just a friend. I only met her a few days ago. And she just came by to drop off my sunglasses! That's all. There's nothing between me and Liz."

Then I look up and see Liz by the front door, with the backpack over her shoulder and a funny look on her face. "Sorry" is on the tip of my tongue, but what's wrong with what I just said? We *aren't* dating. We *are* just friends. She knows I'm interested in Serafina. She's my spy! Anyway, before I can say anything, she turns and walks out.

"Oh," says Mrs. B. "So it was *another* girl you went to the party with?"

Luckily, Mr. B rescues me before this gets any worse. "Here you go," he says, handing me a mop. "Bucket and soap in that cupboard over there. Aspen!" He hands a wet rag to his son. "You let those dogs in the yard, so this is your fault too. Go and help Justin clean up."

I never thought mopping a floor and scrubbing mud out of sofa cushions could feel like so much of a relief.

And that's it. I thought I was probably in for a few more lectures about paying attention to my job or having girls over, but the Beltons seem to think that everything's been said. I try to keep a low profile for the rest of the afternoon. And that evening, I make sure that the door of my room is firmly closed before I call Serafina.

Calling Antonio's beforehand was definitely a good move. I mean, Jack's was fine for the first date. But after seeing Carter's house—well. That's the kind of thing Serafina's used to. I can't let her think that going out with me means nothing better than hot dogs on the beach all the time.

When I tell Serafina that reservations have already been made, all she can do is say yes. Tomorrow night, seven o'clock.

I go down to the computer to update Alex and Dillon on my progress, and try to ignore my mom's e-mail about Neil. I'm describing Carter's party, minus the shirt and salsa incident, when an IM pops up on the screen.

queenelizabeth *(9:38:09 PM)*: hey justin. u get in real trouble?

justintime (9:38:56 PM): No, they were cool. I just had to clean up the mess, and Aspen had to help.

queenelizabeth *(9:39:16 PM)*: pretty lucky

justintime (9:40:21 PM): Would have been more lucky if I remembered to close the door. But thx for helping out. You were great.

queenelizabeth *(9:39:16 PM)*: anytime

justintime (9:40:21 PM): Listen, I'm going out with Serafina again tomorrow night. To Antonio's.

queenelizabeth *(9:40:50 PM)*: antonio's? y there?

justintime (9:41:49 PM): Because it's never mind anyway what do you think I should talk about with her?

queenelizabeth *(9:42:37 PM)*: how should i know? whatever comes up i guess.

justintime (9:42:02 PM): Thanks for the help.

queenelizabeth *(9:43:26 PM)*: sorry it's just it's not a script u know. talk about whatever she brings up, what's on your mind. what IS on your mind?

justintime (9:44:19 PM): What's always on a guy's mind when he's around girls.

queenelizabeth (*9:45:38 PM*): well don't talk about THAT. not on the 3rd date.

justintime (9:45:54 PM): just joking

queenelizabeth (*9:46:14 PM*): LOL

justintime (9:46:49 PM): Can I ask you something?

queenelizabeth (*9:47:13 PM*): u just did

justintime (9:47:51 PM): Ha. I mean, about yr family?

queenelizabeth (*9:48:15 PM*): what?

justintime (9:49:02 PM): You really don't mind yr dad's girl-friend?

queenelizabeth (*9:49:54 PM*): no I really don't. y are you all interested in this?

justintime (9:50:33 PM): It's just never mind

queenelizabeth (*9:50:56 PM*): no y?

justintime (9:51:52 PM): My mom's dating some guy. She's all excited.

queenelizabeth (*9:52:45 PM*): so? isn't that good?

justintime (9:53:59 PM): I guess.

queenelizabeth (*9:54:24 PM*): u so don't mean that

justintime (9:56:03 PM): I'm supposed to be happy for her, I know. But it's weird. She always talks about my dad like he was the best guy on earth.

queenelizabeth (*9:57:13 PM*): fina told me about yr dad. sorry.

justintime (9:59:14 PM): It's not like I miss him or anything. I never even knew him. But I guess I don't like the idea of her dating somebody else. Not seriously.

queenelizabeth (*10:01:08 PM*): how long ago did yr dad die?

justintime (10:02:04 PM): When I was 3.

queenelizabeth (*10:03:23* PM): 13 years. long time for yr mom to be all alone.

justintime (10:04:17 PM): She's not alone. I'm there.

queenelizabeth (*10:04:51* PM): not this summer

justintime (10:05:46 PM): Well, that's great too, isn't it? Like she was just waiting for me to move out before she hooked up with some loser. Sorry I put such a cramp in her social life.

queenelizabeth (*10:07:17* PM): whoa. want to take a break until the hostility settles down? go outside and break some windows or something? kill a few puppies?

justintime (10:19:33 PM): sorry

queenelizabeth (*10:22:52* PM): OK me too. maybe it's harder for u than for me. my mom left right after the twins were born. i was glad to see her go.

justintime (10:23:17 PM): hostility?

queenelizabeth (*10:26:37* PM): hey u didn't know her. i don't know why she had kids in the first place. she never wanted any of us. used to hear her on the phone, complaining to her friends about how much work it was to take care of a kid, how she was tired of it. i said I'd take care of Annie and Ellie so they didn't grow up feeling like that.

justintime (10:27:24 PM): That's terrible really sorry.

queenelizabeth (*10:30:16* PM): don't know why people have kids if they don't want them. same with the McGraws. Max is such a cool little kid but they hardly spend any time with him. like he's too much trouble just for existing. don't get it. y have kids if you don't like kids?

justintime (10:31:48 PM): Know what you mean. That McGraw guy seemed like a jerk.

queenelizabeth (10:32:15 PM): yeah. imagine Carter all grown up.

justintime (10:32:46 PM): Don't want to imagine that.

queenelizabeth (10:34:25 PM): i stay out of his way mostly. anyway that's why I don't mind Mel. maybe not the person i'd pick for a best friend. but she's good with A&E. they love her. she's good for my dad too.

justintime (10:35:16 PM): OK I get the message.

queenelizabeth (10:36:21 PM): no message. u just asked why I don't mind Mel & I'm answering.

justintime (10:36:59 PM): OK

queenelizabeth (10:37:38 PM): listen I better get off the computer. the McGraws think I spend too much time online.

justintime (10:38:23 PM): OK later

queenelizabeth (10:38:47 PM): thnx

I sit there at the computer, thinking about what Liz said. About thirteen years being a long time for my mom to be alone.

She's right, I'm *not* there this summer. And in a few years I'll be away at college, working on the prelaw degree. So I can see that, yeah, maybe my mom would want to have somebody in her life about now.

I can see it. But it doesn't make me feel any better.

I think you'll really like him when you meet him, she said. Yeah, right. We'll get on great. He'll probably want to be my *friend.* Take me to baseball games. Give me fatherly advice.

And the thing is, he's not—

—dammit—

—he's not my *dad.*

Okay, so I never knew my dad. Okay, so it's kind of crazy for me to miss him. But I guess I got kind of used, in a weird way, to *not* having him around. To this empty space in my life that I can fill up with what my mom tells me about him, what I imagine he was like. And now there's this new guy, and he's all ready to step into that space, and that means I'm going to lose the one tiny piece of my dad that I have left.

At five minutes to seven on Monday night, I stash Mr.
B's bike around the corner from Antonio's so I can walk up
to the entrance. I borrowed a tie from Mr. B as well as the
bike, and I pause before I go inside to check my reflection in
the glass door. Dockers, white shirt, Wall Street power tie. I
didn't have Aspen in the kiddie seat, of course, so I don't
have to worry about helmet hair. All right. Here we go.

Serafina's sitting on a padded bench by the door. Her
white dress makes her glow in the dim light.

"Hi," I say. "Sorry if I'm late."

"No, I just got here." She gets up, and the dress swirls
against her legs. What other girl can make standing up look
like a dance move? I tell the hostess we have reservations, and
she takes us to a table way back in a corner. Who cares? It's
more private here. I hold Serafina's chair for her, just like I
imagined.

We're the youngest people in this place by an easy thirty
years.

I wish I could order a bottle of champagne, like that Neil
guy did for my mom. Instead, I ask for Coke, she gets iced

tea. The waiter brings us menus, and we both read them intently, like we're afraid somebody's going to come up and snatch them out of our hands.

Then I look over at the prices. If Serafina wants an appetizer and a main course and dessert, it'll make serious inroads into my first week's salary. I skim for the cheapest entrée.

All Serafina wants is a salad. I sigh silently with relief and ask for pasta with shrimp.

Then we sit some more. Serafina picks the lemon out of her iced tea and squeezes it.

Why can't I think of anything to ask her? Maybe it's just that it's so *quiet* in here. People are leaning over their tables, talking like they're brokering illegal stock deals and don't want anybody to hear. The waiters pick up each piece of silverware separately, so it doesn't clink. It's kind of like having a date in a funeral parlor. No wonder I can't come up with anything to talk about. All this silence is smothering the ideas in my head before they can get out of my mouth.

"I saw Carter yesterday," Serafina says.

Oh, damn.

"He thinks Liz is very clumsy."

She's smiling a little.

"Liz isn't clumsy," I say.

"I know. Liz is very brave."

"You should have seen the look on his face," I tell her. "Liz dripped ice cream all over that car, and he looked like she'd murdered his firstborn child." Wait a minute. She used to go out with this guy. Which I'm not supposed to know. "Sorry. I mean, I know he's a friend of yours . . ."

"No, not really. He doesn't have many friends."

"He's got all those people always hanging out with him." She shrugs.

"He has a car. And he throws parties when his parents are out of town. And . . ."

"And . . . ?" I don't know why I'm pushing this. I should just be happy that she doesn't care about me almost getting into a fight with her ex.

"And I don't know. People just do what he says. Sometimes it's like that."

I can't help thinking it wasn't like that with Liz.

The candlelight makes Serafina's face soft. She has makeup on, dark red lipstick, eyeliner that makes her eyes look wide and deep.

I've never seen Liz wearing makeup. Of course, I've never seen her dressed up for anything. If I'd taken Liz to Antonio's, would she have worn lipstick? A dress?

Who cares what Liz would wear? I try to snap myself out of this. I'm here with *Serafina*. Not some skinny, bossy girl who dresses like a construction worker.

Our food comes. Serafina nibbles at a leaf of frilly lettuce. I stab a shrimp and wrap spaghetti around it.

"You are very quiet tonight," Serafina says. "You look at me, but you don't say anything."

"You won't believe what happened yesterday," I say quickly. "There are these two little dogs next door and . . ."

I make it into a good story. Dogs, mud, Aspen chasing Yippy and his Navy SEAL around the living room. Serafina's smiling.

"And I'm about to grab hold of the couch and heave it across the room when Liz comes out of the kitchen—"

"Liz was there?"

Wait a minute. How did Liz get back into this conversation?

"Yeah, she came by. With my sunglasses. I gave them to her at the pool, and she forgot . . ."

"I see."

She eats a crouton. Is she mad? I realize, too late, that it sort of sounds like Liz and I have been spending the last few days in each other's hip pockets. It hasn't been like that. It's just that I kept running into her . . . and we kept talking . . . and sending IM messages. . . .

This is ridiculous. It's like I've suddenly lost all my dating skills. Pretty soon I'll be picking my teeth with my fork and wiping my nose on a napkin. I try to get a grip on myself and ask her stuff about Molly, her job, school, movies, music. She answers. She asks me a few questions back. At least we're not acting like we're embalmed anymore. But it still doesn't feel like it did on our first date, when we were sitting on the beach, and it seemed so easy to talk to her.

The waiter whisks our plates away while I'm still chewing on my last bite. I get the feeling he thinks I'm not going to be a big tipper.

"Do you want something for dessert?" I ask her.

She thinks about it. Then she leans forward, elbows on the table, and whispers at me.

"Can we go to Jack's for ice cream?"

An excellent plan. Jack's was the site of our first date. I'll definitely be able to talk to her at Jack's, once we get away from this mausoleum of a restaurant.

She drives. I'll come back for Mr. B's bike later.

Jack's is crowded. Lots of kids standing in line to order food at the windows, or sitting at the picnic tables, or hanging around the parked cars. I check. No dark red convertible. Carter must be getting it cleaned and pressed.

Turns out Serafina doesn't want ice cream after all. Of her own, that is. She wants a bite of mine.

"Ice cream is too fattening," she explains, licking chocolate peanut-butter crunch off her upper lip.

She looks so cute doing it I can't help grinning. This date is going to turn out okay after all. Somebody props a car door open and cranks up the radio. Everybody claps. I guess the DJ decided to go retro tonight, because some guy is singing about his Sharona.

"Fina!" Somebody swoops by our picnic table. It's Kath, the redhead. "Oh, hey, Justin. Fina, come on, we want to dance. You know everybody will do it if you start."

"Justin, do you mind?" Serafina asks me. "Just for one song."

Of course, I have to say that I don't mind. And sit there on top of a picnic table with my feet up on the bench, watching her move off with her friends. Under a streetlight, she stands there, smiling. She starts to move her hips to the rhythm. Then her shoulders and arms join in. She shakes her head so that long, loose, black hair ripples down her back. It's nice to watch, I have to admit. Only it'd be nicer if some tall guy with slicked-back hair wasn't dancing so close to her. And if she wasn't smiling at him and matching her movements to his.

Someone sits down on the picnic table next to me. I look over and see that it's Liz, eating a hot dog.

"So, you lied, huh?" she says.

"What?"

"Thought you liked to dance. Disco fever and everything."

Oh yeah. "Right. I lied. Sue me." Serafina does a spin that makes her skirt flare out. People clap. "Go ahead, though. If you want to dance."

"That's okay. You look like you could use some company."

What's that supposed to mean? Now I'm a charity case? "No, I'm fine. If you want to . . ."

"Fina just likes to dance, you know."

"Yeah, I know. Sure. I don't mind."

"Right. That's why you look like you want to kill somebody, and you're sitting there letting your ice cream melt?"

Her superior tone is annoying, but I'm too busy licking chocolate off my fingers to retaliate.

"So who is that guy anyway?" I say casually, once I have the ice cream situation under control.

"His name's Marcus."

Just for one song, Serafina said. But a new song has come on, something Latin with a quick beat, and Marcus has his arm around Serafina's waist. They twirl around like it's a ballroom dancing competition. He dips her.

"Seriously, Justin," Liz says. "It's always like this with Fina, every summer since we were thirteen. You think you're the first guy to fall for her? She's always going to get attention. You just have to get used to it."

Get used to it. Get used to some tall guy swinging my girlfriend around? Nobody said dating a Hamptons girl was supposed to turn me into a doormat.

The song ends. Serafina waves good-bye to Marcus and heads back over to me.

"That was fun!" She tucks a loose strand of hair behind one ear, smiling big. "Hi, Liz. Justin, I could teach you to dance. It's not hard."

"You think I could learn to be as good as Marcus?"

"Justin!" Liz snaps at me, like she's my mom or my teacher or something.

"Marcus is very good," Serafina says. "Can I have a bite of your ice cream?"

Now she wants my ice cream too. I take her out, I sit and watch her dance while some other guy puts his hands all over her, and now she wants my sweet and creamy dessert? Well, fine.

"Sure. Have it all." I push the sticky cone into her hand.

"I don't want—"

"Go ahead, take it. Why should I care?"

"Justin, what is wrong?"

I barely notice Liz slipping off the picnic table and backing away. Coward. Well, I don't need her around to make my point with Serafina.

"You said just one dance. That was two."

"I didn't think you would mind."

"I wouldn't *mind*?" I hear my voice go up and pull it back down. If you have to explain to your girlfriend what she did wrong, it's best not to attract an audience. "You thought I wouldn't mind if you spent half the night dancing with some other guy?"

"Two songs is not half the night."

"Right, fine. I thought we were out on a date, that's all.

But if you'd rather hang out with Marcus, go ahead. Feel free."

"All right."

She says it perfectly calmly. And then she turns around and walks back toward the parking lot, tossing my ice cream cone into a garbage can along the way.

GREAT MOVE."

I spin around. Liz is standing behind me, looking at me. What is this, the peanut gallery? I can't even have a fight with my girlfriend without Liz watching every move and commenting on it? Next thing you know there'll be a Web site: "Justin and Serafina—What's Next?" Should Serafina have danced with Marcus? Was Justin right to get angry? Click to vote and register to receive e-mails with exciting new offers to interfere in Justin's life!

"Don't start, okay?" I take off for the street to walk back to Antonio's and pick up Mr. B's bike. But Liz isn't about to quit. She's walking right next to me, talking in my ear.

"So, did you plan to break up with Serafina tonight? Or was that just a spur-of-the-moment thing?"

"What? I didn't break up with her!"

"Really? You just yelled at her in public. You always do that with girls you're trying to impress?"

"She shouldn't have gone off dancing with that guy. You don't think I had a right to be pissed off?"

"That's just Fina and guys. I tried to tell you. Anyway, there's no way Marcus is interested in Fina."

"He sure looked interested to me."

"He already has a *boy*friend, genius."

Oh.

I discover that my feet have stopped walking. Liz is looking at me like I'm an idiot. I guess maybe I *am* an idiot.

You'd think Serafina had never heard of sarcasm. I didn't mean she should go hang out with Marcus, even though I told her to. I meant she should stay and hang out with me. You'd think any girl would know that what I told her to do was the exact opposite of what I wanted her to do.

I mean, wasn't it obvious?

This was supposed to be so easy. I met Serafina on my first day here. And she's perfect. Nice, gorgeous, rich. So what's going on? Why is this so much harder than I imagined?

"You think she's really mad at me?" I ask Liz.

"At a guess—yeah. Probably."

Shit. "What should I do?"

Liz rolls her eyes. "Honestly, do they raise guys under a rock or something? Apologize, dingbat."

"That's it?"

"For real, though. Girls are suckers for a guy who knows how to apologize. But you have to mean it." She flaps her hands at me like she's shooing away a chicken. "Go on, what are you standing here staring at me for? I swear, I don't know why I bother helping you out at all. Who knows who she's dancing with right now? Hurry up!"

I'm hurrying.

Serafina's not dancing with anybody. She's standing around near the cars with some of her friends, talking. I hover on the edge of things for a minute.

Everybody stops talking. They look at me.

"Uh, hi." A smooth and suave opening line if there ever was one.

Serafina turns to look at me. "Hello."

She's definitely mad at me. Calmly, politely, seriously mad.

"Can I talk to you?"

She shrugs and nods, then follows me away from her friends. When we're by ourselves, she looks at me and lifts her eyebrows. Waiting.

"I'm sorry," I say.

She lifts her eyebrows again. She's going to make me work for this.

"I'm sorry I yelled at you," I say. "I'm sorry I told you I didn't mind if you went dancing and then got mad about it."

Serafina seems to consider this for a moment. Then she sighs.

"Let's walk down to the beach," she says.

Is that forgiveness or not? I follow her down the little path to the sand. She sits down on an old tree trunk that washed up years ago. I sit beside her, facing the water.

"I'm sorry too," she says. "It's too bad our date ended that way. It was a very nice restaurant."

"A little quiet, though."

I glance at her sideways. She's smiling. This is progress. A girl can't stay mad at a guy once he's made her laugh. It's one of the rules.

"And we would have fit in better if we had gray hair," I go on.

Score. She laughs.

"So," I say. "Can we just wipe this date off the scoreboard? Start all over?"

"I don't think so."

That's not what she's supposed to say. That was a first-class apology. And I got her to laugh. She's not supposed to still be mad. What gives?

"Look, I said I was sorry. I mean it. Really."

She turns around on the log to face me.

"Justin. I'm not angry at you. But I don't think this is working out. You and me."

What? No, no, no. This is *not* what's supposed to be happening.

"Look, really. I didn't mean—"

"I like you, Justin. Really. But you are too serious for me." That stops me cold. "It's summer, you know? I just want to go out on some dates. Have fun. And besides, I don't think this is really what you want either."

What's that supposed to mean?

"You keep spending time with Liz."

"Liz?" I practically choke on the word. First Mrs. B, now Serafina, thinks there's something going on between me and Liz? "We're just friends. Really, Serafina, nothing happened with me and Liz. If you think—"

Serafina smiles gently at me. "I know that. But you keep talking about her. And it wasn't hard at dinner to guess that you were thinking about someone else. I think you should tell her how much you are thinking about her." She gets up, smooths down her dress, and leans over to kiss me on the cheek. "Thank you for dinner, Justin. I'll see you later."

She walks back to Jack's and the other kids, leaving me sitting there, staring at the water. All that really cold water.

After a while I get up and walk back up the path, across the parking lot, along the street, and back to Antonio's to pick up Mr. B's bike. Then I ride back to the Beltons'.

It's funny. I feel like I should go into the den, turn on the computer, and IM Liz. Tell her what happened. Ask her what to do.

But obviously, I can't do that. And I don't feel like talking to Dillon or Alex. Alex, all happy with his new girlfriend. And Dillon, who would just say "I told you so." *You always get too serious, Blakewell. Scares them off.*

So I just go to bed. It's not even ten o'clock yet. But what else is there to do?

Tuesday I take Aspen to the pool.

I mean, Liz isn't my type. She's skinny and bossy and she dresses like a boy. She's not even pretty.

Wednesday I take Aspen to the beach.

Well, okay. So Liz has that blonde hair with the nice highlights, so light they look sort of silver in the sun. And those eyes, almost the same blue as her swimming suit.

But she's not in Serafina's class.

On Thursday I take Aspen to the park.

And Liz just does whatever she feels like. She never thinks about how crazy she looks. She'll take a cannonball off the dock or drop ice cream on the leather seat of a convertible.

And she didn't think twice about helping me out. With Carter. With Yippy and Yappy. With Serafina.

It's funny. Here I was, trying as hard as I could to date Serafina. But it wasn't Serafina I wanted to talk to about my mom and Neil.

On the other hand, Serafina's definitely gorgeous. And a world-class kisser. And pretty smart too.

Smart enough to figure out which girl I really like, even when I was being pretty dumb about it myself.

On Friday evening, about nine o'clock, the phone rings.

It's Serafina. She's calling from downtown. She asks if I can meet her there in front of the coffee shop on Main Street.

Liz just called her, all upset. It seems Max has run away.

Chapter 19

LIZ COMES TEARING UP ON A BIKE just a few minutes after I get to the coffee shop, where Serafina is waiting. She skids to a stop and gets off to tell us what happened, standing there with her hands jammed deep in her pockets, her whole body tense.

"Mr. McGraw promised Max he'd take him to get some ice cream after dinner," she says. Each word sounds sharp, like it's been filed to a point. "But then he didn't feel like it. He said he was tired. When Max started to cry, he sent him to his room. I said I'd stay and play with him, but it's my night off, and McGraw told me to just go. I went down to Jack's to hang out. But I got cold and went back to get a jacket, and when I checked in on Max, he wasn't there."

The way she looks, McGraw would have much worse than some ice cream on a leather car seat if Liz had her way.

"All right." Serafina is still calm. "Where would he go, do you think?"

"I don't know." Liz is frowning. "Mr. McGraw took the car to look for him. But I thought a bike would be better. You could pretty easily miss a little kid in the dark if you're just driving by."

"We'll all look," Serafina says. "Justin has a bike too, and I have my car. Where should we start?"

"On the beach, I think. He loves it there."

"Let's look by the dock," Serafina suggests. "That's where he usually plays."

There are still a bunch of people on the beach, even though it's getting dark. We dodge around them, looking behind the dock pilings, calling out, "Max!" But there's no sign of him. We start walking down the beach, asking everybody we pass if they've seen a kid by himself. Nobody has. Liz rubs her eyes hard with the back of her hand.

"He's okay," I tell her. "I'm sure he is."

Now she looks like she's angry with me too. "You're *sure*? How are you sure?"

"I just . . ."

"It's been more than an hour. What if he's not even on the beach? What if he went into the water? He could have been kidnapped. He could—"

"Hey!" I interrupt her before this gets too bad. "And he could be just fine. Let's wait until we have a *reason* to think something terrible happened, okay? Let's just look for him right now. That's the important thing. If you keep thinking about what might have happened to him, you can't concentrate so much on looking. All right?"

I'm just talking, just trying to interrupt the chain of horrible images running through her head. But to my surprise, what comes out of my mouth actually makes sense.

"Justin is very right," Serafina says seriously.

We keep looking.

Liz goes up to a tall guy who's got his back to her. "Excuse me, have you seen . . ."

I check behind a clump of grass big enough to hide a four-year-old. Nothing.

When I look back, Liz is still talking to the tall guy. He looks familiar.

Oh, great. This is all we need right now. It's Carter.

I can't hear what they're saying, but I see Liz take a step back, shaking her head. I start walking over so I can punch Carter out if I need to. Or even if I just sort of want to. I can see Serafina over Liz's shoulder, still asking people if they've seen a little boy with blonde hair.

". . . get my attention," Carter is saying to Liz as I come up to them. "I knew what you wanted with that ice cream thing. But don't mess with my car, baby."

Liz looks disgusted. "Get a grip, Carter. Your attention is the last thing I want."

"That's not what you said last summer." Is he slurring his words just a little bit? "That party. My place. Remember?"

"I remember you were drunk, and I did you the favor of not kicking you where it counts."

"*What* about last summer?" I'm a little slow picking up on what's going on here.

"I don't have *time* for this crap." For some reason Liz is glaring at both of us. "I'm looking for a little kid, Carter. That's actually more important than your ego. Come *on*, Justin."

She starts off down the beach. I follow her. But I'm still trying to figure out what Carter meant about last summer. Has he been hitting on Liz too? As well as Serafina? Is he after every girl in the Hamptons? Or just every girl I like?

"Hey, last summer . . . ," I start to say to Liz.

"Justin, I will kill you if you bring that up right now."

I think she actually means it. Then Carter comes up behind us.

"*What?*" Liz spins around.

"Hey, nothing." He holds out empty hands in front of him, all innocent. "Just thought you'd like to know—that kid you take care of?" He points. "He's over there."

Max is at one of the tables outside Jack's. Jack is sitting next to him, patting him a little awkwardly on the back. Max has a dish of ice cream in one hand and a spoon in the other, and he's digging in with every appearance of enjoyment.

Liz takes off across the sand. By the time we get there, she has Max up in a great big hug. He's holding on to her with both his legs and arms, like a giant spider, and has his face buried in her shoulder.

Serafina takes the cup of ice cream out of his hand so it won't drip any more down the back of Liz's shirt.

Jack is shaking his head. "I'm glad somebody showed up for him. I was about to call the police. Wouldn't tell me his name, wouldn't tell me his phone number. I kept asking if he didn't want his mommy or his daddy, but first all he'd say is he wanted ice cream, and then all he'd say is he wanted Liz. You Liz?"

Liz nods, holding tightly on to Max.

"You work for the McGraw family, don't you? That's their little kid?"

But Liz is talking to Max. "Max, honey. Don't ever run off like that. You scared me to death. What're you doing here?"

"I want ice cream!" Max wails, and bursts into tears.

Liz sits down with him. "I know you do, honey, I know,"

she murmurs. She doesn't try to make him stop crying, just rocks him gently back and forth. "It's okay now. Shhhh, it's okay."

"Liz," Serafina says, digging her cell phone out of her purse. "What is the McGraws' number? I'll call and let them know he's all right."

Liz keeps on rocking Max, but she looks up over his head, and her eyes are narrow and furious.

"Mr. McGraw gave me his cell," she says coldly. "I'll call him in a minute."

"But they are worried—" Serafina holds the phone out.

"Let them worry." Liz puts her cheek down on top of Max's head. "First I'm going to make sure Max is okay."

After a little while Max stops crying. I go and get a handful of paper napkins from the counter. Max lets go of his death grip on Liz and sits up straighter on her lap, and she dries his eyes and makes him blow his nose.

"Okay, baby?" Liz asks, looking at him carefully.

Max snuffles and nods.

"Don't *ever* do that, you hear me? What did you come here for?"

"Wanted Liz," Max says. He sounds like he's getting sleepy.

Liz looks like she might start to cry herself. Instead she digs in her pocket to pull out the phone. But just as she's dialing the number, there's a screech of tires from the street. A shiny blue SUV pulls into the parking lot and a man jumps out.

Jack comes back out of the Shack.

"Had to call," he says quietly to Liz. "You don't fool around with somebody's kid."

Liz stands up slowly, holding Max in her arms, as Mr. Mc-Graw runs toward her.

"Liz! Max! Is he—"

"He's fine," Liz says. Max holds on to her shirt as she tries to hand him over. "No, Max, honey, go to your dad."

McGraw squeezes Max tightly. He puts his face in Max's hair like he doesn't want anybody to see his expression.

I really feel sorry for him for a minute.

It only lasts a minute.

"Why didn't you call?" McGraw asks, looking up. "I gave you a phone, Liz."

"I was just going to," Liz says, holding out the phone to prove it.

"You found him, when? Ten minutes ago? Fifteen? Why didn't you call right away?"

"He was upset," Liz says. I flash back to the time McGraw picked Liz and Max up at the beach, the way Liz defended herself then. This is the same—no expression, a flat tone of voice. No emotion at all.

"*He* was upset? What do you think I was? What do you think his mother was?"

"Max was crying," I say. I can't just stand there and let him yell at Liz. "Liz couldn't call you and take care of him at the same time."

"Stay out of this," McGraw tells me and turns back to Liz. "That's enough, Liz. I can't take any more irresponsibility from you."

"That's not fair!" I can't help jumping in again. Liz is just standing there, not saying a word. Somebody has to get in the way of this. Irresponsible? Liz? How irresponsible is it to break a promise to a kid? How irresponsible is it to get your four-year-old so upset he runs away? "Max came down here looking for Liz. *She's* not the one who did something wrong."

The look he turns on me is actually scary. I have to stop myself from taking a step backward. And I realize that we've collected quite a crowd around us.

McGraw realizes it too.

"Go home," he says to Liz. "Tomorrow you can come by the house and pick up your things." His voice is poisonous.

I'm not sure how much of this Max is taking in, but he sure gets that his father is angry. He starts to squirm in his arms and cry.

"I'm taking Max home," McGraw says. And he walks off. Liz slowly sits down at one of the picnic tables. We can hear Max sobbing all the way to McGraw's car. Nobody can think of what to say.

Chapter 20

MY MOM AND NEIL are driving off in Carter's dark red convertible. They were supposed to pick me up, but they forgot. If I ran after them, shouting and waving, they'd see me and stop, but I can't, because Aspen is missing and I have to go look for him. And Liz is being no help at all. She's putting on lipstick, looking in a mirror. "I'm sure he's okay," she says.

I get so mad at her that I wake myself up. The sheet's twisted around my legs, like I was fighting with it in my sleep.

Just a dream. It didn't mean anything. I'm not going to think about it.

Just like I'm not going to think about what Carter said last night, about what might have happened—*did* anything happen?—between him and Liz last summer. Liz isn't dumb enough to have fallen for anything Carter had to say. I know that. I'll just stop thinking about it. Right now.

I've got plans for today, and I'm not going to let a stupid dream or a jerk like Carter spoil them. Today's the day I start dating the right Hamptons girl.

Maybe it's the way that dream made my heart race, or

maybe it's the idea of finally telling Liz how I feel about her, but after a while I have to admit that I'm not going to fall back asleep. I throw on some clothes without bothering to shower and head downstairs to the den to check my e-mail.

Nothing from Alex or Dillon. One from my mom.

To: justinb597@webmail.com
From: Lblakewell@walkerandco.com
Subject: Checking In

Honey—
Everything okay? Haven't heard back from you in a while.
love,
Mom

I hit REPLY. But then I get stuck. I can't figure out what to say.

I know I'm supposed to be happy for her. I get that. I didn't need Liz to remind me that my mom's been alone a long time. And I have to admit, when it comes right down to it, that I don't want to be the one to wreck things for her. I mean, if she said, *Sure, honey, since it makes you uncomfortable, I'll quit seeing the only guy I've liked in thirteen years*—I guess I'd feel pretty bad about that.

But that doesn't mean I'm about to throw Neil a ticker tape parade either.

So I can't say I'm thrilled, because I'm not. I can't say what I really feel, because that would hurt my mom. So what, exactly, am I supposed to say?

Hey, Mom, nice going. Glad to see you've still got the moves.

Listen, Mom, couldn't you do better than someone with a dweeby name like Neil?

Gee, Mom, that's great that you're replacing my dad with some guy I never even met.

Impossible. I close the e-mail. It's almost breakfast time anyway. Maybe this evening I can think of some way to answer. Right now my mind's a blank and my stomach's growling.

In the kitchen, Mr. and Mrs. B are drinking coffee at the counter and talking about the McGraws and what happened last night. I didn't tell them anything. But Mrs. B was on the telephone early this morning. Gossip travels faster than the speed of light.

Of course, she was talking to other adults, so she got the adult version, the one where the teenager is, obviously, wrong.

Aspen wants to make scrambled eggs, so I get out what we'll need and pull a chair close to the counter for him to stand on.

"I don't like Peter McGraw," Mrs. B is saying. "But I have to admit I can't argue with him here."

I give Aspen an egg. He smacks it enthusiastically on the edge of the bowl. I get a paper towel for his yellow, slimy fingers and fish half the eggshell out of the bowl. Hope nobody minds if breakfast comes out a little crunchy. After I pour in some milk, Aspen picks up a fork and starts beating the eggs. I get a good grip on the bowl before it dances off the counter.

"There's no excuse for that girl not calling right away," Mrs. B goes on.

"You weren't there," I say, before I can stop myself.

"Excuse me?" Mrs. B says. I can tell I'm on thin ice here, and I might have learned something from watching McGraw and Liz last night. Teenagers are always wrong, adults are always right, especially when it comes to little kids.

It's like when Liz was over here before. Just because I'm a guy and Liz is a girl, Mrs. B assumed I must have been making out frantically with her and ignoring Aspen. Now she's assuming Liz wasn't doing her job. And that's not right. She doesn't even know Liz, or what happened last night.

And anyway, Liz is about to become my girlfriend. That means I have to stand up for her.

"Her name's Liz," I say. "And she was going to call him. She only waited a few minutes so she could calm Max down. He was really upset."

"Liz," Mr. B says. "Isn't that the girl who was over here earlier?"

I should probably take this as a warning that the conversation can only go downhill from here.

"Nevertheless, that's irrelevant," Mrs. B says. "Whether Justin knows her or not, the girl was wrong in not calling right away."

"Her name's Liz!" I say again. Aspen stops beating the eggs. Clutching the fork, he stares at his parents and me. "And okay, even if she was wrong for five minutes, what about the dad? His kid ran away from home *to* Liz. So how come all anybody can talk about is what *Liz* did wrong?"

They're looking at me, startled. Mr. B clears his throat. "Well, Justin—"

But I'm on a roll. I can't wait for him to finish.

"I guess it's because you can fire nannies and not parents,"

I say, and throw down the dish towel that's lying across my shoulder. "I don't want any breakfast." I leave Aspen standing on his chair by the counter and slam the front door behind me.

My anger gives me so much energy that I'm walking down the street before I know what I'm doing. The Beltons are pretty good people, and they've been decent to me, but the first time any question comes up about a teenager, a nanny, and an adult, of course they line up on the adult's side. Not a question. Not even a minute or two to find out the other side of the story.

And there's a little thought in the back of my head that won't shut up, reminding me that the Beltons lined up not just on the side of the adult, but also on the side of the adult who's rich.

It's so easy for them to assume that McGraw is right. Even if he's a jerk. Even if he's mean to his kid. Still, he's one of them. Wall Street. Summer cottage. Power ties. So he must be right and "the girl"—they wouldn't call her Liz even after I told them her name—must be wrong.

I'm not paying attention to where I'm going, and when I look up, I realize I'm on the street that runs along the beach, the one where Carter lives. I'm about to turn around—all I need to make this morning perfect is to run into that guy—when I see Serafina ahead of me, leaning against her little green Honda. She gives me a smile when I come up.

"Hello, Justin."

She sounds just like she always did. Not a hint that a couple of days ago she broke up with me.

"What's going on?" I ask her.

"I'm waiting for Liz." Serafina nods toward the house she's

parked in front of. Right, Liz said the McGraws' house was just down the road from Carter's. "She needed a ride back home."

So this is the McGraws' "cottage." Three stories, a stained-glass window over the front door, a garden out front that must use up half the state's water resources.

I lean against Serafina's car too. We wait for a little while. Then the door to the McGraws' house opens and Liz walks out. She has a suitcase in one hand and a backpack over her shoulder. And she walks quickly to the car. No looking back.

"Hey, Justin," Liz says quietly. "I didn't know you were coming. Thanks for the ride, Fina."

It doesn't seem like the moment to tell her I just stumbled on Serafina's car by accident.

We drive away from the shore, away from the big houses with the front porches and the manicured lawns. Liz stares out the window. I sit hunched up in the backseat.

"Sorry about you losing your job," I say. "That McGraw guy—"

"Let's not talk about it, okay?" Liz says, not looking around.

After a while Serafina puts the radio on. We listen in silence until at last we pull up at a small, shabby brown house on a block of small, shabby brown houses. There's a beat-up, kid-sized bicycle lying on its side next to the front walk and a swing set in the backyard.

Liz and I get out.

"I have to get back and watch Molly," Serafina says, and waves out the window as she drives off.

I pick up Liz's suitcase before she can get a grip on it herself. That gives me an excuse to follow her up the walk.

At last. Now I'm going to get a chance to talk to her.

This was supposed to be such a great summer. But lately nothing's been going the way I expected. Serafina broke up with me. I just had a huge fight with my employers. My mom's dating someone she actually likes.

But Liz is the one thing I'm sure about. This, at least, I can make come out right.

"Thanks. I got it," Liz says when we get to the front door. She reaches over for the suitcase.

I was kind of hoping she'd invite me in. But I guess that can wait a minute.

"So," I say. "I'll see you around, right? This summer?"

"Sure." She doesn't seem all that enthusiastic about the prospect.

"We can hang out."

"Yeah. Maybe you and me and Fina can go to a movie or something."

This isn't really going the way I envisioned it.

"I meant, just the two of us," I say. "Something a little more . . . intimate."

She turns to stare at me. "You mean a *date?*"

"I mean . . . yes," I say defiantly. Why should she look like I've offered to infect her with polio? "A date. With me, yeah."

"But you're with Serafina," Liz says, looking a little panicked. "I was helping you with Serafina."

Loyal to her friends too. Another good quality.

"Not anymore," I say. "We broke up." No need to get into inessential details about who broke up with whom.

Liz still looks shocked, so I try to explain some more.

"It kind of surprised me too," I say. "I mean, Serafina's everything I thought I wanted. She's beautiful and nice and—" I'm about to add something about how, if kissing were an Olympic sport, Serafina would make the team, hands down, but maybe that's not exactly where I want to go right now. "And I didn't think of you that way at first. We were just friends."

"I know," Liz says. She's not smiling for some reason, like she still doesn't quite get what I'm saying. "You were pretty clear on that when I was over at the Beltons'."

"Yeah, but it just took me a while to know what I want. I mean, you're not the type of girl I normally fall for."

"You like them beautiful and nice. And rich."

"Usually," I agree. "But this time—I don't know, Liz, there's something about you. It doesn't matter about the way you dress and everything. It took me a while to figure it out. But you're the one I want to be with."

She looks at me, a slow smile lighting up her face, and falls into my arms.

I mean, that's what she should have done. That's what she was supposed to do. But apparently she hadn't read the script.

"Well, good," she says. "Congratulations." It's impossible to miss the sarcasm.

"Congratulations? What for?"

"For finally figuring out what you want. That must be a big relief."

What is she talking about? Is she mad because it took me a while to realize that she's the girl for me?

"Look, I'm sorry I waited so long. But we can start going out right away. Tonight, if you want."

"Oh, we can?"

Why is she acting like this? She doesn't even look happy.

"Yeah, we can. Why not?"

"Well, for one thing, you haven't asked me yet."

Oh. Rewind. I wouldn't have thought Liz was so into formality, but if she wants to do it by the book, that's how we'll do it. I'd even go down on one knee if that's what she wanted.

"Liz," I say. "Will you go out with me tonight?"

"No."

You know how, when you're going downstairs in the dark, sometimes you think you've reached the last step but there's one more? How your foot goes out and it feels like you're falling a hundred feet, even though it can't be more than twelve inches?

It feels like that.

"What do you mean—" I start to ask, and then stop myself. No. She means no. It's pretty obvious. What do I need, a translation?

"I mean no." See, perfectly clear. "What did you think? That I was just sitting around waiting for you to ask me out when you finally figured out that you like me, even though I'm not beautiful and not nice and not rich and not really your type? Gee, thanks. I'm so flattered that you like me in spite of everything that's wrong with me."

What a minute. I didn't say any of that. I didn't say she wasn't pretty. Or nice. And, hey, she's *not* rich. What happened here? "Look, I didn't mean—"

"Listen, Justin. I'm not some little townie who can't wait to get asked out by a guy from the city."

"I never said—"

"Yeah, I know." She sighs. "Forget it." She picks up the suitcase, gets a key out of her pocket, and turns her back on me to open the door.

I just stand there. Like I've forgotten how to move my feet.

"Justin?" With the door half open, she turns around to look at me. "Thanks." For a second I think this means she's changed her mind, that she'll go out with me after all. But she goes on. "For last night. For standing up for me with McGraw."

"Sure," I say, like an idiot. "Anytime." Like she gets publicly fired once a week or so.

"You need a ride back into town? Maybe I can call Mel. Borrow her car while she's at work."

So I get turned down by a girl and then accept a ride from her? What would we talk about on the way into town? The mind boggles.

"No thanks!" I say loudly. I may not have a girlfriend or much prospect of one for the rest of the summer. But I do have some dignity. I'll walk.

I don't get why Liz is still standing there in front of the open door. I asked her out, she said no. Aren't we done? But she seems to think there's still something more to be said.

"Look, Justin. You're a nice guy." Anytime a girl says this, you can bet what follows isn't going to be good. "It's just—if I wanted to go out with a guy, it'd be one who actually *asked* me on a date, instead of just assuming I couldn't wait to go out with him. And who maybe even thought I was pretty."

"Like Carter?" I say, really nasty all of a sudden. "I guess Carter thought you were pretty last summer."

My ears can't believe how stupid my mouth just got.

Liz's face goes very still.

"I don't want to go out with Carter," she says quietly. "Or anybody like him."

And she goes inside and shuts the door behind her.

Chapter
21

JUST AS I'M DISCOVERING that a twenty-minute car ride converts into about a three-hour walk, a guy in a pickup truck offers me a lift. I ride the rest of the way to the rich part of town in the back of the truck, surrounded by boxes of strawberries.

Pete the strawberry farmer drops me off on Main Street, and I walk the couple of blocks back to the Beltons'. It doesn't occur to me until I'm halfway up the front steps that Liz might not be the only one who's out of a job.

Yelling at your employers, slamming out of the house, leaving your kid halfway through making the scrambled eggs—this is not behavior that's recommended in the manny handbook.

Aspen and his parents are sitting in the living room. Mrs. B's flipping through a magazine. Mr. B's sitting on the floor, playing War with Aspen.

"Justin!" Mrs. B says as I walk in.

I can't tell from her voice if she's angry or upset or what. She's just staring at me. I don't get the look on her face. I don't know what I'm supposed to say.

"Justin!" Aspen yells, and he runs to me, scattering cards across the floor. He barrels into me, and I fall against the doorframe.

"Hey, buddy, easy," I say, and put my hands on his shoulders. He looks up at me.

"Are you still mad?"

Now I really feel like a jerk. However I felt about Liz, making a little kid worry is not something to be proud of.

"No, I'm not mad anymore," I tell him, and look over at his parents. If somebody's mad in here, it's probably them.

"Aspen, go to your room for a little while, please," Mrs. B says. Mr. B gets up off the floor.

Here it comes.

Aspen doesn't want to go, but Mrs. B's using her lawyer voice, and he goes. I try to look cool and unconcerned. It's just a job. So what if I get fired? There are plenty of other jobs. I'll just have to slink back to New York with my tail between my legs and admit that, not only did two girls turn me down, but I also got fired after two weeks. No sweat. Nothing to worry about.

I don't think I'm doing very well at looking cool.

"We were worried about you, Justin," Mrs. B says.

They were?

"Don't just slam out of here like that again," she says, frowning at me. "Aspen was frightened."

"I'm sorry," I say. I don't like apologizing. And I don't think I was all the way wrong. But I do feel bad about scaring Aspen. "Really. I didn't mean to get Aspen upset."

Mrs. B nods.

Nobody says anything.

"So . . . do I still have a job?" I ask.

They both look like I've suddenly started speaking Sanskrit.

"Of course you do!" Mr. B says.

"Justin, Aspen loves you," Mrs. B says. "And you do a great job with him. We just want you to talk to us next time if you're that upset about something. What made you think we were going to fire you?"

"Well, just . . . that McGraw guy fired Liz, and you thought . . ." I can't figure out how to finish that sentence.

Mrs. B looks a little embarrassed.

"I want to apologize for that, Justin. I made a decision before I heard all the evidence. I'm sorry."

What do you know. An adult admitting she was wrong.

"It's just—that's a parent's worst nightmare. Someday when you have kids, you'll know how it feels to worry like that."

I remember how I felt at the pool, when I lost sight of Aspen for two minutes. And I'd only known him for about a week. Then I remember how McGraw held on to Max when he got him back.

"Okay," I say. "Maybe Liz should have called right away. But she really didn't wait more than a few minutes."

Mrs. B nods. "And maybe Peter McGraw should have admitted that some of what happened was his fault. And maybe I should have listened to you. All right?"

All right.

Everybody stands around for a few minutes, looking relieved but with nothing more to say.

"I'll, uh, go and play with Aspen," I say.

That's my job, after all.

Aspen's got Legos spread out all over his floor.

"Want to build a space station?" I say, looking down at him.

"Yeah!" he says, grinning.

One thing about this kid, he doesn't hold grudges. We stack the Legos up high. He builds a lumpy-looking rocket ship, and I build a launch pad. The rocket takes off with a lot of throat-mangling sound effects.

I hope this space mission goes better than the manny mission. Let's face it. Alex has a girlfriend. Dillon has several. My mom's getting all dewy-eyed over Neil. Even Yappy has Yippy. And I'm sitting on the floor with a four-year-old, playing with Legos.

"Can we go to the beach?" Aspen asks.

"Sure. After you clean up your Legos."

Aspen throws the rocket ship into a red plastic bin. I scoop up a few handfuls of Legos to help him out.

"And you have to jump off the dock," he tells me.

"No way."

"Way."

"Go get your bathing suit."

Aspen jumps up and runs out of the room, yelling, "Way way way!" Then he turns around, runs back, stops in the doorway, looks at me, and lets out a terrific belch.

I give him a thumbs-up, and he runs off.

At the beach, Aspen and I go through our usual full-body workout—wave jumping, hole digging, and of course, repeated sprints up and down the sand. Then I sit him down to refuel with some animal crackers and a juice box. He sucks so hard on the straw he practically turns his head inside out.

A few yards over to our left, a pretty blonde girl, her face flushed red, is arguing with a little kid who doesn't want sunscreen on.

"You *have* to have it," the girl says, sounding a little frantic. "You don't want to get sunburned, do you?" She tries to smear a fingerful of white goop on the kid's nose, but he's too quick for her.

"No!" he bellows. Amazing how a sound that loud can come out of such small lungs.

There's an extra box of juice in my backpack. "Here—try this," I say, and toss it over. The blonde girl looks up in surprise.

"Distraction," I explain. "I bet you can get the sunscreen on him while he's drinking it."

Sure enough, as soon as the kid starts sucking on the straw, he quiets down enough to let the girl smear sunscreen all over him.

"Hey, thanks." She looks at me gratefully. "Next time I'll bring something for him to drink."

"And animal crackers," I say. "Never go anywhere without animal crackers."

Speaking of animal crackers, I look over to see how Aspen's doing with his snack and discover that he's asleep. He's flopped over in a little lump on the towel, still clutching the empty juice box in one hand. I pry the box out of his fingers and drape another towel over him so he won't get sunburned. Nothing much to do now but sit here and admire the view.

And think.

This was supposed to be the perfect summer. Let's see where it's gotten me so far.

Financial situation: dire. Between the dinner at Antonio's and the money I'm going to owe my mom for the shirt I can never wear again, I'm showing very little profit for my first two weeks.

Romantic situation: ditto. The rich, gorgeous, sweet-tempered girl broke up with me, which was okay because it meant I could go after the girl I *really* like. But that girl turned me down flat.

Family situation: not so hot either. My mom's embracing the wonderful world of dating, and I can't seem to cheer from the sidelines.

Well, the romantic stuff is out of my hands. Liz made it clear she doesn't want me around. Nothing I can do about that.

The financial mess is beyond repair too. I can't get back money I've already spent.

But it's just occurred to me that there's at least one thing I can do to fix stuff with my mom.

The whole problem has been that I can't tell her I hate the idea of a new guy in her life—and therefore in mine. And I can't tell her I'm happy about it either.

But the thought comes to me now, like a lightbulb going off inside my head—why not? Why can't I tell her I'm fine with it even if that's not true? It's not exactly a brand-new concept. It's called lying.

I'm supposed to be happy for her. So I'll just *act* happy. I'll fake it so well she'll never guess what I really feel. And so what if I'm not exactly, perfectly, 100 percent ecstatic myself? My mom will be happy. That's the important part. That's what matters most.

I'm feeling pretty good about myself as I dig the Beltons' cell phone out of my backpack. If they gave out medals for being a perfect son, I'd be at the top of the list. Saint Justin, that's me. I dial my mom's number and let it ring.

"Hello?"

"Hey, Mom. It's me."

"Justin! The prodigal son calls at last. Where've you been, at the beach?"

"Yeah, I guess."

"You don't sound that excited about it."

"No, it's fine. I just wanted to tell you something."

"Okay. Shoot."

"About that guy. Neil."

"Oh?" Now she sounds a little worried.

"I don't mind."

Silence.

"I mean, it's okay. I felt a little weird about it at first. But you *should* be going out. Meeting guys. You're still young and pretty good-looking and everything."

"Well. Thank you. Shall we notify the Mature Miss America Pageant?"

Oops. Better hurry on to the next point. "And I'm going to be going to college pretty soon. So I just mean, I understand if you'd like to have somebody around. Get married or whatever. I think it's great. Really. Seriously. Great."

"Hold on there." I hear her put a hand over the mouthpiece and say to somebody, "Just give me a minute, okay? Can you go call the elevator?" Then she's back. "Justin. Look, this isn't the best time."

"Is he there?"

"Well—yes. We're going to lunch."

"It's okay." I have to grit my teeth a little to get this out, but I accomplish it. "You can go."

"Don't you think you're going a little fast here, hon?"

Huh?

"You're expecting me to *marry* Neil? This is only our fourth date!"

But she sounded so happy. So sure about him.

"Sure, I like him. But let's not rush things here. We're just having fun, seeing if we really like each other. You never know. Anything could happen. But relax. I'm not about to bring you home a new stepfather right at the moment."

Oh.

"Justin, I've got to go. He's waiting. Everything all right?"

"Sure," I say. "Great."

"We'll talk some more."

"Okay."

"Love you."

"Okay."

She hangs up. I turn off the phone and put it away.

I have to admit, it's kind of a letdown. After psyching myself up to give her my blessing, it's a shock to find out she doesn't actually want it.

A shock . . . but not really in a bad way.

No new stepfather at the moment. Nobody showing up and trying to be my new dad. Just my mom having some fun. Seeing if she likes this guy and if he likes her back.

I feel kind of emptied out. Like my brain doesn't know what to do with itself now that it doesn't have Serafina or Liz or my mom to worry about anymore.

I lean over and shake Aspen awake. "C'mon, buddy. Time to go home."

He snorts and mumbles.

I toss all of his gear into the backpack and scoop him up in one arm, a heavy load of sandy, sweaty, sticky little boy. His head flops against my shoulder as I carry him toward the parking lot.

Down the beach, past the old dock, I can see a skinny girl with blonde hair so light it looks silvery in the sun. She's too far away for me to see her face, but her bathing suit is a familiar shade of faded blue.

It might be Liz. But I don't go over and investigate. For one thing, Aspen's pretty heavy. For another, she made it clear that I'm not her favorite person at the moment.

So I just stand there for a minute, watching her. Just this morning, I thought I had it all under control. I thought I'd picked out the right Hamptons girl at last. I wish I knew what went wrong.

Well, I guess I do know, I think, as I start walking again. What went wrong is that girls never go according to plan. Even my mom all of a sudden turns out to have a life of her own.

Maybe instead of law school I should go into psychology. Then I might be able to predict what girls are going to do.

But probably not.

I'm just about to the parking lot when I start smiling to myself.

So girls never go according to plan. But you know, guys don't either. Liz probably thinks she got rid of me for good. But I don't think it's going to be that simple.

She told me so herself. Girls are suckers for a guy who knows how to apologize. I'll let her cool off for a few days. Then show up at the door with some flowers. Tell her I'm sorry and mean it. And see where things go from there.

Maybe she'll kick me out again. Maybe we'll just be friends. Maybe something more.

The manny mission isn't really over. I've still got two weeks in the Hamptons. It's like my mom said: You never know.

Anything could happen.